Lullaby

of

Lake Charles

May unexpected paths lead you to joy - always!

Lullaby

of

Lake Charles

Nancy

Nancy Cadle Craddock

This is dedicated to my

Louisiana friends

and family.

Geaux Tigers!

*Sometimes the road of life
takes an unexpected turn
and you have no choice but
to follow it to end up in the place
you are supposed to be.*

Unknown

1

Meteorologists predicted that the disturbance in the Atlantic would head back out to sea since it was so early in the hurricane season.

Instead, it moved steadily toward the southern tip of Florida where it entered the Gulf of Mexico.

There it stayed, growing stronger and more deadly over the warm Gulf waters.

Comparisons filled the airwaves between Katrina and the newly named hurricane – Gabby.

Even the city of New Orleans seemed to take note. Cars headed across Lake Pontchartrain toward Mississippi and out of harm's way.

In the end, Gabby passed the Big Easy with only a minimum of wind damage.

Instead landfall was made in Vermillion Parish midway between

Intracoastal City and Grand Chenier, roughly two hundred miles west of the Big Easy.

The hurricane weakened as soon as she hit land. Even so, Gabby continued spinning tornadoes in every direction, leaving a trail of rubble, twisted cell towers and overturned vehicles as far north as Lafayette all the way to Lake Charles.

Miraculously, there were no reported deaths.

Only later, would Louisiana come to know, lives were changed just the same, as gusts of wind continued to blow.

2

Margaret lifted her Louboutin from the gas pedal and steered her shiny gold Mercedes past the fist-out, thumb-up skinny girl on the narrow shoulder of Interstate 10. Pressing on the brake, she bit her lip.

To be truthful, it wasn't the forlorn-looking girl in the faded jeans and torn t-shirt that brought Margaret to a stop. It was the dilapidated Mustang the girl was leaning against. With the gold stripe running across the car's black hood, it was identical to her husband Paul's sporty one during their dating years.

Fear and doubt made Margaret's heart beat faster as a couple of eighteen wheelers zoomed past but rising thoughts of fleeing were put to rest when the out-of-breath skinny girl got closer to Margaret's car. Too late. Margaret was stuck.

Worse yet, she'd made an uncomfortable discovery a couple of miles back.

Either her cell phone was dead or service hadn't been restored so soon after Gabby hit land. Probably the latter.

Not that it mattered but Margaret had left her phone charger back in Baton Rouge, along with many unspoken fertility questions on the faces of her mother and two sisters.

Margaret pulled down her visor and glanced in the mirror while tucking a couple of shoulder-length strands of wavy blonde hair behind her ear.

After adjusting the mirror to see behind her, she noted there was nothing but the broken-down car and swampland behind her.

The girl tapped on Margaret's window.

Tentatively, Margaret lowered it, wishing she'd kept going toward Houston and the comfort of her husband's arms.

Instead, here she was, in the middle of nowhere, high above Louisiana's mosquito infested Atchafalaya Basin with a stranger leaning in her car window.

***

Paul swiped his card across the keypad to the right of two enormous carved walnut

4

doors. Shifting his electronic notebook and smart phone to his other hand, he waited for a familiar beep.

Seconds later, one of the skyscraper's ornately carved mahogany doors automatically swung open and Paul stepped into a huge foyer.

Once inside the architectural firm of Jackson, Burke & Connelly, Paul knew it would be only a matter of thirty minutes-or-so before the calmness of the early morning erupted into its usual hub of activity and chatter.

Sleek chrome chairs and glass end-tables were placed with precision around an enormous atrium.

The foyer was motionless except for brightly colored fish that glided effortlessly in a two story floor-to-ceiling aquarium that had been featured in several architecture magazines.

As always, Paul took a couple of minutes to watch the fish while enjoying the sound of the waterfall at the far end of the room.

Moving again, Paul's Italian shoes. made sharp staccato clicks as he crossed the highly polished black and white marble floor and ducked behind several large Fichus trees. There, he punched in his code to gain access to the private elevator that would carry him to the top floor, high above the tangled web of Houston's never-ceasing traffic.

From the foyer to his office, Paul's thoughts were on Margaret. He always missed her when she was away.

Paul's office was surprisingly sparse for such a vital, active person. Since being moved from a smaller space to the highly prized large corner office, he'd been so engrossed in the design of Holland's Openlander Arts Center, he hadn't paid much attention to what was lacking in his own surroundings.

However, he was very aware that his move from a smaller, windowless cubicle indicated his firm was very pleased with him and the number of clients he alone was responsible for bringing to the company.

Paul checked his watch and gathered everything he needed for his first presentation of the day. All was in order except his favorite photo of his smiling wife which had slipped down in the silver frame on his desk. He made a mental note to fix it later.

Now wasn't the time to think of anyone or anything except securing the men who would be arriving soon as prospective clients.

***

The girl's words came out in a rush. "Thanks for stopping. One of my tires busted wide open. Wait here until I get my baby? Okay? Gonna take a couple minutes to unhook her car seat and gather up stuff."

Margaret nodded, but the girl was already running back to the Mustang.

For safety, Margaret wedged her Hermes bag between the edge of her seat and the driver's door before poking her head out the window to get a better view of the Mustang.

The young girl disappeared headfirst into the car's backseat. Minutes later, she surfaced with a bundle of squirmy pink.

A baby, a real-live baby.
Not an egg in a Petri dish.
Not precisely filled-out adoption applications on the counter.
Not a maybe-someday baby.

A here-and-now baby.

3

Margaret flipped on the blinker and steered her Mercedes back on Interstate 10, using more caution than usual.

Now that there was a baby in the car, Margaret felt a responsibility to make sure the gorgeous little pink bundle of shamrock-green eyes and whisper of auburn hair made it safely home.

The young girl in the passenger seat brushed the darkish hair from her eyes. "My name's Clover Applewood, what's yours?"

Margaret must have looked a bit shocked because the girl immediately said, "I know, strange name, but my mama never did go for being ordinary."

Margaret nodded with a smile, as if naming a child "Clover" was a good thing.

The girl continued, "But hey, my friends call me Chloe, so I guess it works. What's your name?"

"Margaret Sinclair."

The girl didn't answer so Margaret glanced toward the little pink goddess in the tattered car seat and asked, "What's her name and how old is she?"

"MacKenzie. Named her for my Ma."

In her rear-view mirror, Margaret watched a tractor-trailer that was rapidly gaining on them. "Bet your mom is crazy about her granddaughter."

Chloe looked straight ahead and said in a flat tone, "Ma's dead."

"Oh, I'm sorry. And your dad... if you don't mind me asking?"

"Never knew him. Anyways... MacKenzie and I do fine, just fine."

Margaret felt a wave of pity for the strangely-named girl beside her. She doubted they made out "just fine" but answered "I'm sure you do" just the same.

When it became apparent the girl had no response to that, Margaret repeated, "How old is MacKenzie?"

"Eight months yesterday," Chloe answered with a smile.

"She sure is beautiful," Margaret replied. And she was. Margaret studied babies everywhere – the mall, restaurants... everywhere. Without a doubt, MacKenzie had them all beat with her huge green eyes, creamy complexion and soft auburn hair.

Margaret thought it was a striking combination, and one you didn't see often.

The baby whimpered and Chloe was quick to turn around. "Be good, MacKenzie. We don't want this nice lady to put us out on the side of the road, now do we?"

Nice lady. With a start, Margaret realized she was the nice lady Chloe was talking about. Thirty-three must seem really old to the young girl, who couldn't be more than sixteen, maybe seventeen.

Margaret glanced at Chloe and back over her shoulder at the yawning baby before giving her attention to the rapidly approaching eighteen-wheeler behind her.

Chloe cleared her throat. "I really appreciate you giving us a ride. Wasn't sure how MacKenzie and I were going to get to Lake Charles. How far you goin', anyways?"

The eighteen-wheeler thundered past, claiming the fast lane for himself.

Margaret kept her eyes on the road and didn't loosen her grip on the steering wheel until there was a bit of distance between the truck and her Mercedes.

"I'm on my way home to Houston but I can drop you off in Lake Charles on the way. No problem."

Chloe smiled. "Must be my lucky day."

"Mine, too." Margaret returned Chloe's smile but studied the young girl

11

from the corner of her eye every chance she got. Definitely not a day over seventeen.

No jewelry.

Not even a wedding band.

Margaret looked in her rear-view mirror to make sure no one else was barreling down on them. The road was wide open.

No parents.

No husband.

No future.

Glancing toward Chloe again, Margaret wondered how someone so young could possibly afford to raise a baby.

Babies took a lot of money and from the look of the rusted-out Mustang with its worn-out tires, not to mention the shabby clothes both the girl and her baby were wearing, money was a problem. A huge problem.

Margaret realized she'd need more time to learn all that she could about the young mother riding beside her and there were only so many miles between the interstate over the murky waters of the Atchafalaya Basin and the small sleepy town of Lake Charles.

Margaret slowed her car, going just fast enough to stay with the flow of the occasional car or two.

The slower things went, the better to keep focused on everything ahead of her and she might need every mile.

4

The fading summer azaleas of Margaret's childhood home were a couple of hours behind her. Now even the Atchafalaya Basin was disappearing in her rear view mirror.

Margaret again glanced at the young girl beside her and had a fleeting thought of the familiar sights, sounds and smells of her own not-too-distant youth; bonfires on the Mississippi River levee, the reverberation of "Geaux Tigers" in her feet as thousands cheered and stomped their beloved Tigers to victory, and the smell of bacon and grits that often lured both she and Paul to the Student Union at the start of classes on the much loved campus.

Margaret's thoughts of the past evaporated as Chloe pointed to a blue "Rest Area" sign ahead. "Can we stop?"

"Sure. If phone service has been restored, do you want to make a call to someone about your car?"

"Later maybe. My friend Eddie will come back for it. He's a mechanic and a tow-truck driver, so it won't be a problem." Chloe twirled a strand of her long hair. "I wouldn't mind making a bathroom stop though."

Margaret glanced at the sleeping baby and then met Chloe's sad-looking eyes with a smile. "I wouldn't mind a break either."

Minutes later, Margaret flipped on her blinker and guided the Mercedes down an exit ramp, coming to a stop in front of an old metal water fountain.

Chloe unbelted the sleepy baby as Margaret turned the ignition off. The baby opened her enormous eyes which now an even more vivid green in the bright sunlight.

Before opening her car door, Margaret grabbed her keys and a rubber band before shoving her purse under her seat. The air was humid as she climbed out. In a matter of moments, Chloe and MacKenzie were by her side.

Chloe chewed on her bottom lip as the three of them neared the restroom. "Do you mind holding MacKenzie while I run in?"

Margaret put her car keys and rubber band in her jeans' pocket and smiled her most reassuring smile. "Sure. No problem."

Chloe handed MacKenzie to Margaret and sprinted toward the restroom. "Don't go anywhere," she called over her shoulder, "I'll be right back."

Margaret smiled. Wrapping her arms around the auburn-haired baby felt like holding Cotton Candy, fluffy and wonderful.

Margaret hugged MacKenzie even closer as the baby squirmed and then nuzzled against Margaret's neck.

Instinctively, Margaret kissed the baby on the top of her gorgeous little head just as Chloe was emerging from the bathroom door.

Margaret wasn't sure if Chloe had witnessed the kiss but thought it was a possibility. Wanting to put the girl at ease, she "You probably think I'm nuts kissing your baby... but that's something we all... my family... does. We kiss babies on the top of their heads. We all do. Um... it's like a tradition... or something."

Chloe stared straight ahead. "And people let you get away with that?"

Margaret tried not to blush. *Cheeky kid.* Worse, Margaret thought she heard Chloe mutter "Rich People!" but since she wasn't sure, she didn't bother to answer. The

17

last thing she wanted to do was cause friction between the new mother and herself.

Chloe lifted the small baby out of Margaret's arms, leaving Margaret engulfed in a familiar feeling of despair and loss.

Once again, there was an empty void where a baby should have been.

Fighting back tears, Margaret said, "I need to splash a little water on my face. Be back before you know it."

Chloe pointed toward a cement picnic table under an oak tree with hanging moss. "We'll be over there."

Margaret made her way down the sidewalk to the ladies' bathroom.

Using her rubber band, Margaret pulled her highlighted hair into a twisted pony-tail of sorts and splashed water on her porcelain face.

Once again, she could kick herself for leaving her phone charger in Baton Rouge. She needed to hear Paul's voice. She wanted to hear she'd done the right thing – picking up the scrawny girl and her baby.

Even if your phone was charged and cell towers were working, Margaret knew a phone call was out of the question.

Today was the reason Paul wasn't with her in the first place. This was the morning Paul's newest investors were hopefully going to sign contracts on several large jobs, including an Anguilla multi-villa resort. Deals like this didn't come along often and Paul didn't need to be distracted.

Back outside and under the glare of the sun, Margaret caught sight of Chloe and the baby. Carefully, she made her way across the patches of bare ground to them.

MacKenzie had fallen sound asleep.

"Out like a light," Margaret remarked.

"She's been a good baby right from the start."

Margaret nodded. "Still, even a good baby is a lot of work, and you're so young."

Chloe looked up at the sky. "I told you... we do fine."

"I didn't mean just MacKenzie, *all* babies are a lot of work."

Still looking skyward, Chloe answered, "The school guidance counselor said if I was old enough to make a baby, I was old enough to raise one."

"Still... you're young and have the rest of your life ahead of you and so does the baby's daddy, if he's your age."

Chloe laughed. "There's no baby-daddy. Just me and MacKenzie."

"What about that friend of yours... Eddie?"

"What about him? He's a friend. A good one, but just a friend. At least, he doesn't act like he's ashamed to be seen in public with me like T…" Chloe voice drifted off.

Margaret bit her lip. "T-who?"

"Never mind."

Margaret was desperate to learn more. Another person in the mix could change things. *What* things exactly, Margaret wasn't quite sure. "Is this T-person MacKenzie's daddy?"

Chloe's voice quivered when she answered, "Yes, but he's out of my league, that's for sure."

"And Eddie?" Margaret ventured to ask.

"I guess he and I might end up together… maybe." She added with a laugh, "And uh, I appreciate the ride and all, but I don't usually share my personal business with strangers."

Margaret looked straight at Chloe. "Well, you never know what the future holds. Maybe we'll end up more than strangers."

"I doubt it," Chloe whispered, running her fingers through MacKenzie's auburn hair. Turning toward Margaret, she added, "My Granny was religious. If she were alive today, I'd bet she's say this is one of those times to 'Trust and Obey'. You a believer?"

Margaret nodded, but didn't feel the urge to add that she'd never had the need to express her beliefs sitting in a pew beside strangers. To be truthful, doubt about a benevolent "supreme being" always crept in whenever she heard some awful story about an abused or molested child.

Margaret often felt estranged from a God who would give a precious baby to unfit parents and deny her and Paul one.

Paul saw things differently. His philosophy was when the right sperm hit the right egg, a baby was sure to follow.

In her mind, Margaret knew he was right, but her heart... well, that was a different matter. Her unanswered baby prayers were beginning to wear on her. She was thirty-three years old and certainly not getting any younger.

And here was Chloe with the cutest baby in the universe. What was fair about that?

Still, Margaret reasoned, the young girl was far from having it all.

No father.

No mother.

No baby daddy.

How could someone so young be so alone?

Margaret kept her tears at bay as she pulled her necklace, the one with a small gold cross, outside of her blouse and stood up, ready to proceed.

Maybe God had plans for Margaret after all.

21

5

Back on the highway, traffic was sparse. Margaret clicked on the Cruise Control and turned on her satellite radio. Minutes later, the smell of a poopy diaper filled the air, followed by a loud wail.

Chloe sighed. "Guess we're stopping again. Sorry."

"No problem."

Margaret slightly raised the volume on the radio but the music didn't distract MacKenzie who continued to cry as they sped toward the next exit.

Chloe unhooked her seatbelt, turned and talked softly to MacKenzie. "Don't cry, baby, Mama gonna find you a bottle and change your diaper... if I've still got any."

Great. Margaret bit her bottom lip to keep from saying what was on her mind. *Doing just fine. Definitely not.*

At first, MacKenzie's wails softened as Chloe talked, but in no time at all, they were back to the high shrieks they'd been in the first place.

"Hang in there, MacKenzie. We're going down the off-ramp," Margaret shouted over the baby's jagged cries.

Unfortunately, the exit didn't offer much hope, only a sketchy-looking gas station, a run-down fruit stand and an out-of-business tire rotation place that had JESUS SAVES painted in purple across the front window.

Margaret brought the car to a stop in the gravel driveway of the fruit stand. "Guess we need to get back on the highway. Maybe we'll have better luck there."

Chloe pointed in the direction of a small country church barely visible from the road. "Go there."

"A church? Why there?" Margaret asked, pressing on the gas.

"Churches are rarely locked and someone always leaves a clean diaper, or two, in the church nursery."

"Oh," Margaret answered, pulling into the church lot. "And the milk?"

Chloe was half-way out of the car when she answered. "Wait here. They may have a makeshift kitchen with a refrigerator or something."

Margaret turned to make sure MacKenzie's diaper wasn't leaking. That kind of stain on the car's soft beige leather would be hard to explain to her Junior League friends.

Luckily, everything in MacKenzie's diaper was staying there.

Hoping to distract the crying eight-month-old, Margaret searched her mind for a lullaby to sing. All she could come up with was *The Wheels on the Bus* which quieted the baby for all of about six seconds.

Margaret thought if the whole thing wasn't so nerve-wracking, it would be downright funny.

Before Margaret reached the verse about the wipers on the bus, the rear car door opened and Chloe jumped in, holding up three diapers. "Jackpot."

"You've got to be kidding!" Margaret exclaimed.

Chloe laughed as she lifted MacKenzie from the car seat and placed the baby in her lap. "Viola!" she exclaimed as she pulled a travel-size container from her pocket. "Wipes, too!"

Quick as a wink, Chloe managed to get MacKenzie's diaper off without a smudge of poop anywhere.

For the first time in a long time, Margaret threw back her head and burst out laughing. *You had to hand it to the young mom.*

Chloe had wisdom beyond her years, or maybe it was what Paul called "street smarts".

Unfortunately, even with a clean diaper, MacKenzie continued to cry.

Chloe kissed MacKenzie's right cheek. "Love you, baby girl. Now, we're gonna find you some milk."

Margaret tucked an escaped strand of hair from her pony-tail behind her ear. "Maybe we'll find a fast-food restaurant."

"Hey, I've got an idea. We're only a mile or two from Queenie Dubois's place. Let's go there. Her daughter, not Kizzy, the other one, was expecting around the same time I was pregnant with MacKenzie. She's bound to have an empty bottle she can fill up for MacKenzie."

Margaret tried not to frown. *Queenie Dubois? Kizzy? Who were these people?*

Chloe placed a whimpering MacKenzie back in her car seat. "I bet she'll see us coming and have a bottle ready when we get there."

Trying to lessen the tension in her back and neck, Margaret shrugged her shoulders several times and rolled her head from side-to-side.

No mother.
No father.
No baby daddy.

But now... someone named Queenie, her pregnant daughter, and another daughter named Kizzy. What kind of a name was that?

In hopes of masking how she felt, Margaret made her voice sound pleasant. "Who is this Queenie DuBois person?"

"Well, I guess you might say Queenie DuBois is like a gypsy... or maybe a Fortune Teller. She can read your palm and see your future in her cards... that kind of stuff. Oh... and... every Saturday night she holds a séance for those with loved ones on the other side."

"Bet she has a big crystal ball, too," Margaret muttered.

"Yep."

Margaret couldn't believe she and Chloe were even having this conversation. Seriously? This was ridiculous. Here Chloe was, poor as the proverbial church mouse, and it was obvious this Queenie DuBois was using some Louisiana Voodoo-Hoodo-something-or-other to coax money away from the single mom. Probably a lot of others, not intelligent enough to protect themselves, too. *Street smart? Yeah, right.*

As if sensing Margaret's disapproval, Chloe piped up. "Me and Eddie, we come here every-so-often."

Margaret stayed quiet.

"Queenie's never been wrong yet. Everything has gone just as she said it would."

Margaret turned to look at her. "Everything?"

Chloe folded her arms. "Well, we're still waiting on the rich lady to give Eddie enough money to start his own business."

"Oh, r-e-a-l-l-y," Margaret said, glad she'd tucked her purse under her seat when they'd left the rest area.

"Queenie never said it was going happen *fast*. Only that it *was* going to happen."

"Did she now? Let me get this straight. This Queenie... this gypsy gal or something... told you and your friend that some rich person was going to hand over a lot of money for your friend to open a business. Doesn't that sound a bit strange to you?"

"Well, it would have, if it was coming from anyone but Queenie. Eddie gets a reading every chance he can and Queenie's never been wrong."

"Hmmm..." Margaret responded as Chloe climbed back in the front seat, slamming the door behind her. "We probably need to get a move on so we'll arrive before flying pigs swoop down from the sky."

"Funny, real funny." Chloe said staring straight ahead.

Margaret rolled her head back-and-forth one last time. "Which way do we go?"

"Turn right and go straight," Chloe muttered, twisting around so that her back was toward Margaret and she was facing the passenger window. "*The Wheels on the Bus.* Really?"

"It was the best I could do." Margaret answered, hoping the gypsy didn't read her.

6

Flakes of faded yellow paint fluttered to the ground when Queenie DuBois slung open her screen door. The wooden porch creaked as she lumbered out of the shadows.

Queenie glanced down the dirt driveway before straightening a dusty hand-painted sign nailed to the front porch banister.

~ Queenie DuBois ~
Psychic Queen of the Bayou

Queenie dusted her large hands together and peered down the driveway again. *Nothing... yet.*

Her index and middle finger tingled. *Two. One taller, or maybe older, than the other.* Itchy palm. *Good. Money coming.* That, she could use.

She turned to go back inside, then stopped. Was that a faint tingling sensation in the tip of her little finger? *Ah... a surprise, A baby, too.*

Queenie already knew the day's reading was going to be anything but humdrum. Hadn't a crow hit her window and died in the early morning light?

Still, not even the faintest sound of a car. No matter. They'd show up soon.

Inside, Queenie put on her multicolored turban.

Staring at her reflection in the once gold-gilded mirror, Queenie reconciled herself to being the bearer of bad news. Unfortunately, there was no way around it.

As Queenie adjusted her headwear, her fourteen-year-old daughter Kizzy looked up from the television. "Reading coming?"

"Yup... 'fraid it's not going to be a good one. C'mon. Get up and help me get things ready. Draw all the drapes and draw 'em tight. And Kizzy, find me some matches."

Kizzy flipped off the television and walked to the windows.

When the room was dark and the matches found, Kizzy turned and tugged on a strand of her short curly brown hair. "Try to get the reading over before *Jeopardy* comes on. Okay, Mama?"

"I'll try, baby girl."

"I just love how the answers pop into my head before Alex Trebek even finishes reading the questions. So totally cool."

Queenie smiled and continued lighting the multitude of candles, all white, on every nook-and-cranny of the sparse furniture surrounding an old wooden table.

Finally, she smoothed out wrinkles on the cranberry-colored tablecloth and placed a fat red candle smack in the middle.

She gave the room one last look, nodded her approval and disappeared behind a faded red velvet curtain into the kitchen.

Queenie then poured herself a tall glass of cold water and called to Kizzy, "There's a baby bottle in that box of things your sister left. 'Spect we're gonna need it. And Kizzy..."

"Yes, ma'am."

"Sterilize that bottle in some boiling water, then you stay close during my readings in case one of ladies feels faint. It probably wouldn't hurt to have a wet wash rag ready, too."

"Okay," Kizzy answered. She was already rummaging through a box of baby things in the corner of her sister's old bedroom.

Queenie scratched her palm and called to Kizzy, "Be ready to pour out a Pepsi, or two, if I ask for 'em."

"Since when we start pouring out Pop during readings?"

"Just do what I say," Queenie said, using one of her ex-husband's handkerchiefs to dab at the small beads of sweat on her forehead. "Sure is hot to only be the first of June."

Kizzy nodded. "Mama, don't forget *Jeopardy* comes on at the top of the hour. Try to go fast."

Queenie didn't answer. Kizzy should know by now that readings paid for the electricity... that ran the television... that *Jeopardy* rolled up on. No, she wouldn't be rushing no readings... now, or ever. That's not how she did things.

The nerves in three of Queenie's fingers were on overdrive. Yet, it was a soft kind of tingling, which only reaffirmed Queenie's inner feelings – females, all.

Rubbing her tingling fingers against her thigh, Queenie walked out on the porch once again and searched the sky for another sign, maybe a buzzard or an ominous cloud. Nothing. Only a dead crow at dawn. *Good. Only one.* She didn't know which one yet, but she'd know the minute the three pulled up.

Like Kizzy watching *Jeopardy,* the answer would pop into her head.

It always did.

***

Paul lifted his finger from the keyboard's built-in mouse pad as the music from the surround-sound speakers softened and the lights came up.

After clearing his throat, Paul scanned the faces of the other seven people around the conference table. Silence. *Good.* His *Power Point* presentations were so stirring, it always took a couple of minutes for prospective investors to recover and get control of their emotions.

Years ago, his secretary remarked she thought the whole room was going to jump up and salute plans for a proposed new dorm on Paul's screen, he was that good.

Paul smiled. He no longer spent his time on small jobs like college dorms. Now, he was designing whole colleges, skyscrapers, museums, and the like. Most of them award-winning. Usually, clients came looking for him. However, every-so-often his firm would come upon a project and secure the perspective investors. Today was one of those days.

As his secretary passed out contracts to the potential clients, Paul opened a large humidor in the middle of the table and lifted out a handful of Cohiba Behike BHK 52s. Expensive. Hard to find.

Gold lighters had been previously engraved with each man's initials and placed within easy reach of all the men at the table.

As the cigars were handed out, clicks sounded throughout the room.

The smell of sun-grown tobacco slowly filled the air as the roomful of millionaires flipped through rather lengthy contracts.

Eventually the men shut their leather-bound contracts and gathered up their gold lighters. No one had to tell these men that cigars are never to be snuffed out. Instead, those with unfinished cigars carefully placed them in Moser glass holders designed expressively for that purpose.

Even though it was early for lunch, instead of inquiring which of the seven men were ready to invest, Paul nonchalantly proposed lunch at The Houston Club. He knew without asking, most would be contacting their lawyers in only a matter of hours to go over the fine details of the contracts.

Now wasn't the time for signing contracts; now was the time for a laid-back, care-free lunch. The kind of meal that said "Hey, if you don't sign on the dotted line, someone else will".

As Paul and the others stepped out in the sunshine, several limousines jumped to life.

After everyone piled into their waiting cars, Paul slid his cell out of his pocket to check his emails. He scrolled through the long list twice, but Margaret's name wasn't there. No text either. *Strange.* Margaret always contacted him when she started for home.

Always.

7

Margaret's usually spotless Mercedes was engulfed in a red cloud of dust as it bounced across the dry rutted ground.

In the bright rays of the sun, chipped and worn-down gravel occasionally glimmered on the reddish dirt.

"Wonder why the soil in this yard looks like Georgia clay instead of what you see everywhere else here in Louisiana?" Margaret muttered.

Chloe shrugged. "Maybe Queenie used her powers to turn her dirt red."

Margaret thought that was the stupidest thing she'd ever heard. "You don't really believe all that hocus-pocus stuff, do you?"

"Just wait. You'll see." Chloe chewed the chipped purple nail polish on the tip of her index finger.

Margaret sighed as she heard a pebble ping the side of her car and dust floated across her windshield.

Margaret glanced at Chloe. "After the long trek out here, this had better be good."

No answer.

Chloe just kept on chewing away the purple polish as if it was the most important thing she'd do all day.

Margaret looked at MacKenzie in the rearview mirror as she slowed to lessen the effects of the rutted road.

As soon as the worn-out driveway ended, Margaret pressed on the brake. Ahead sat a clapboard house. Shotgun style, narrow and long.

The house was yellow; faded in spots to almost white. The roof, which may have started out as green, was now a dull greenish-gray.

Apparently, the trim was in the process of being painted because it was crimson red in some places and dusty rose in others.

Hanging from the ceiling of the rickety porch was an assortment of multi-colored wind chimes and a couple of homemade-looking bird houses.

On the shadowy porch, stood a plump dark-skinned woman against a rusted-out folding chair.

Margaret fought the urge to put the car in reverse and zoom back down the bumpy driveway but Chloe was half-way out the car door.

Margaret made a sideways lunge to put her hand on Chloe's arm. "Chloe, are you sure about this? We've still got a ways to go. Maybe you and your friend Eddie should come back later."

Chloe frowned. "We're here. It'd be stupid to leave. Besides, can't you see? Queenie is waiting for us."

"She didn't even know we were coming so I hardly think she's *waiting* for us."

Chloe squinted at Margaret's face for a moment or two. "You're not afraid are you?"

"Of course not." Margaret answered as she turned the ignition off.

Chloe threw Margaret a smirky kind of smile. "Yeah, right. Come on. Queenie isn't the type to be kept waiting."

Margaret wasn't sure what Chloe meant by that comment but she climbed out and looked around as Chloe unbuckled MacKenzie's car seat.

With MacKenzie in Chloe's arms, the three of them made their way across the dry grass toward the porch.

Once there, the dark-skinned woman didn't utter a sound as she motioned them inside.

Margaret tried not to react and took care not to step near the dead bird that lay on the porch beneath a cracked window.

***

Even on bright sunny days, the inside of The Houston Club was always cool and shady.

The wood-paneled rooms were bursting with museum-quality antique furniture and gorgeous accessories.

The color scheme were ones found in British plaid – dark green, deep burgundy and a touch of navy.

The walls were an art gallery, lined with well-known paintings; many with brass engraved plates stating the names of those who had donated the coveted artwork to the club.

Like clockwork, the once wooden floors were now carpeted every two years. Paul suspected this was more to mask lingering cigar odors than to heavy wear-and-tear.

When city officials banned public smoking in restaurants, it was generally understood that the ordinance didn't extend to establishments like this - ones with deep pockets that got those same city officials elected in the first place.

The long-haired brunette hostess beamed at Paul as she escorted him and his guests to a small private room. After the men were seated, she handed each a crisp one-page menu which changed daily.

There were no prices on the menu. The old saying *"If you have to ask"* certainly applied here.

Paul wondered if any of the men would be surprised to know that most of the steaks were well over a hundred dollars. Not that it mattered, everything would go on the company account.

Paul unfolded his black linen napkin, thinking if all of the contracts were signed, he wouldn't even turn the meals in on his expense account. Heck, with the money he'd make, he and Margaret could eat steak at every meal for the rest of their lives.

Paul smiled to himself, knowing they weren't really steak people. Most of their meals were salads or pasta. Nothing fancy. Often, they scrambled an egg and called it a night.

As the first round of drinks arrived at their table, the conversation flowed.

One of the investors asked if any of the men and their wives would like to attend an upcoming Dallas Cowboys charity auction as his guest. Of course everyone did.

The Houston wealthy were all philanthropists. But why shouldn't they be, Paul reminded himself. Everyone in that crowd was looking for tax write-offs.

To the group, Paul looked engaging, his dry wit adding to the laughter from time-to-time as they talked about their favorite causes and ways to help the less fortunate before the discussion turned to all things golf.

Paul smiled inwardly. The faces changed but the conversation remained the same. As a rule, the rich talked about world affairs. The middle class talked about themselves – where they'd been and what they'd done. The lower class, well, they talked about others.

Yes, Paul thought, faces may change, but people remained the same.

Paul excused himself and made a quick trip to the Men's Room. After tipping the bathroom attendant, he checked his smart phone. Nothing. He sent a quick text to Margaret but there was no reply. Strange. She should have phoned by now, Hurricane Gabby or no Hurricane Gabby.

On his way back to his table, the hostess gave him an "I'm available" kind of smile but Paul pretended not to notice and kept his eyes on the paintings as he walked back toward the others.

This time there was a knot in the pit of his stomach. *Where was she?*

8

Margaret stepped over the badly chipped and rotting threshold onto a threadbare rug.

The rug was devoid of color except for numerous brownish roses woven across it.

The effect was as if a sudden gust of wind had blown in large red roses when someone opened the door and there they stayed, turning a drab brown through the years.

One might have expected a musty smell in contrast to the worn-out rug but Margaret was instantly surprised at a divine fragrance floating in the air.

From Margaret's days behind the perfume counter at Macy's while working her way through school, she could usually identify all the different perfume notes and most scents but she didn't recognize the sugary scent surrounding her now.

Closing her eyes, Margaret enjoyed a feeling of lightness, much like floating.

Several seconds later, the soft cooing of a distant baby along with muffled adult voices brought Margaret back to her surroundings.

She stood still and tried to make-out the words from the other side of a dusty curtain that apparently separated one room from the next.

***

Queenie pulled out a purple wooden chair from the white kitchen table. Chloe sunk down in it, grateful for the thin cotton fabric that hung from the top of the doorframe separating the kitchen from the front room.

Margaret had peered at her all the way there. Why? It was bad enough to look shabby in your own eyes, but it was worse to see it in the eyes of someone else. And what was all that mess with her purse? It was a wonder that rich lady could drive straight for moving it back further and further with her shoe. *Good grief.* It wasn't like Chloe could grab it and run if she wanted. She wouldn't make it far with a baby on her hip.

Queenie cleared her throat. "S'pect yu'ins like something to drink."

"Water please" answered Chloe as Kizzy picked up a goose-decorated glass from the dish-drainer by the sink.

Kizzy turned on the faucet and filled the glass almost to the top. Then, she opened the freezer and plunked in a couple of ice-cubes before handing it to Chloe. "Ere ya go. There's Pop, if'n you want it."

Kizzy scooted a paint-chipped red chair away from the table and sat down.

Chloe shifted MacKenzie to her other arm and picked up the glass. She downed several long sips, noticing for the first time ever that every chair at the table was a different color — purple, red, green and orange. The bright and happy-looking chairs reminded Chloe of the painted doorways in the Quarter.

Without warning, a slender perfectly-manicured hand parted the doorway curtain and in stepped Margaret.

"Well, okay now," Queenie said. "Let's get going. Kizzy, first find t'at baby a toy of some kind. Is the milk warm enough now?"

Kizzy nodded and reached for MacKenzie. "She gonna cry?"

"Doubt it. She's a good baby." Chloe gave MacKenzie a kiss on the head before Kizzy lifted her away.

Kizzy shifted MacKenzie to her other arm as she poured warm milk from a saucepan into a bottle. After twisting on the cap and nipple, she carried a no longer crying MacKenzie out of the room.

Motioning toward Margaret, Queenie said, "Why don'cha hang-out on the porch? There's a chair there and you mi'th even be able to catch yer-self a breeze. Take you a sodee-pop if'n you want."

Margaret shook her head. "Thanks. No soda... but the porch sounds good." She doubted there was any breeze to be had, but at least on the porch she'd be close to her car in case she needed to make a dash for home... away from the stringy teenage mom with her beautiful baby and the strange gypsy woman. Only the girl Kizzy seemed normal, and who was to say if that was an accurate assessment.

Queenie stood up and motioned for Chloe to do the same. "Let's git this show on the road. Yur future's not gonna change just 'cause you're not hearin' it, gu-rl."

* * *

Even if it wasn't break-time, Eddie was tempted to duck out to the side of the garage and give Chloe a call. As he debated whether to chance getting caught by old man Buckley, he remembered Chloe's phone had been disconnected last month. No payment. He'd offered to get the phone turned back on but Chloe asked him to buy formula and diapers instead.

Eddie slid out from under the car and swiped the back of his hand across his forehead, leaving a greasy streak in the shape of a lightning bolt. He stood, arched his back to work out the kinks from being on the low rolling cart with his long legs across the pitted concrete floor.

As he walked to the bin of rusted old tools, he glanced at the clock. Chloe was running late. Eddie smiled. That was one gal that was worth the waiting.

As Eddie sorted through the old tools to find the right size wrench, in walked Buckley. "You're not breaking now are ya?"

"No sir, just gettin' a wrench for the oil-drain plug. Stubborn as all get-out."

Buckley spit tobacco juice in an old coffee can he kept around just for that purpose. "Well, see that you don't strip any screws," he said with a brown stream running down his chin.

Eddie didn't answer as he slung half of his body back down on the cart, and

51

pushed himself under the car. He watched Buckley's worn-out brown shoes shuffle back into his air-conditioned office where he knew Buckley would stay, watching a small black-and-white T.V. for the next half-hour or so, before emerging again to spit out another brown stream.

Eddie tried to ignore the uneasy feeling in the pit of his stomach as he picked up the greasy screwdriver. Chloe should have been back long before now.

9

As soon as Margaret stepped out of the living room and onto the porch, Queenie shut the door behind her. It'd be hot in her small front room but Queenie had built her business on secrecy and she wasn't going to break the rules, even if she was the one who made them up in the first place.

Queenie motioned for the scraggly girl to sit down across from her at the round table in the middle of the room and reached for her notepad and pencil. Queenie liked to warm-up with a bit of numerology. Usually, when she felt a bad reading coming, it steadied her nerves. Besides, pulling out one trick after another seemed to give the client a feeling of money well-spent.

Today was different. For one thing, there wasn't any money on the table so it didn't appear the girl was a paying customer and might be relying on the older lady with her to settle up for the both of them.

Queenie knew nothing would calm her nerves except her bottle of vodka but that would have to wait.

Spitting on the lead point of her pencil was more for show than anything, but Queenie spit just the same. Queenie always had been one for putting on a good show and even though she had a knot in the pit of her stomach, Queenie was hoping she was wrong. And okay, yes, she was stalling for time.

Queenie looked at the girl. "I know you been here before - with a boy. Right?"

Chloe nodded. "You didn't give me a reading, only my friend Eddie. Remember? You told him a rich lady was going to give him enough money to start his own business."

The image of a thin dark-haired man popped into Queenie's head. "That's right. I remember. He didn't seem much older than you."

The girl answered "He isn't" before gnawing on a purple fingernail.

Queenie already knew the answer but she asked mainly to put the girl at ease. "Why haven't you had a reading before now?"

"My friend always offers to pay for me, too, but I don't like to ask him for money unless I need something for my baby."

Queenie cut in, "I see. Well, let's get going. Give me your full name, only first and last. Don't need no middle."

Chloe took a deep breath. "Clover Applewood."

Pencil poised in the air, Queenie asked, "Like the kind of clover you find in the grass?"

Chloe nodded.

Queenie wrote "Clover Applewood" on her pad and gave each letter a corresponding number. Then she injected some addition marks along with an equal sign. She finished by writing an eleven in a circle at the bottom of the page.

Chloe peered at the paper and waited for Queenie to explain.

Queenie smiled. The knot in her stomach was still there... but so far, so good. "Well, 'spect you'd like to know what this-here eleven means."

Chloe returned Queenie's smile. "Sure would."

"According to the charts, you are highly-developed... spiritually."

Chloe wanted to say "Well, whoop-de-do" but stayed silent, and wondered if coming here was a mistake after all.

"You go to church?"

"Not really," Chloe answered.

"Believe in God?" Queenie asked, putting her notepad back in the basket on floor beside her chair.

"Guess so."

"Well, then see, numerology don't lie."

Queenie pulled a long red string from a basket and shaped it into a circle in the middle of the table.

Chloe inched closer.

Queenie made a big show of carefully opening a small velvet pouch. Her eyes never left Chloe's as she gently shook a handful of chicken bones into her other hand.

Queenie cleared her throat. "Now, we're going to see what these-here chicken bones have got to say about you."

"Good stuff, I hope," Chloe replied.

Not seeming to hear her, Queen dropped the velvet pouch into her own lap and shook the bones in her cupped hands, uttering "Bones, bones, snakes alive, this-here girl wants to stay alive".

With a wide swinging motion, Queenie threw the bones on the table. Most landed outside the string circle.

As the bones flew across the table, Chloe flinched. "What do they say?"

"Well, we're only concerned with the ones inside the red circle," Queenie answered. "I was hoping we'd get a wish bone but we didn't."

Chloe searched the circle just in case Queenie had missed it.

The wishbone was not there.

Queenie continued, "Wishbones, they be for good luck."

Chloe spotted the wish bone near the edge of the table, looking like it could topple to the floor any minute.

"Nor did you get a breast bone for love." Queenie picked up the velvet pouch and dropped the bones from outside the circle into its shadowy depth.

Chloe bit her lip. "Well, what do the two in the middle say?"

"This here neck bone stands for poverty. But hey, who isn't poor these days. Nothing new, I bet. Leastwise, not for most people. But lookie-here, we got us a wing bone – travel. Looks like you're going someplace."

Chloe gave Queenie a small smile, knowing the farthest she was likely to go was back home to Lake Charles.

Queenie returned Chloe's smile with a wince. The knot in her stomach had turned into a thousand piercing little pin-pricks. The hardest part about having powers was the knowing of all that was coming.

Queenie reached for her tarot cards with heavy heart, debating whether it would be wrong to send this girl off thinking things were going to be alright or to give her the truth.

Stalling for time, Queenie shuffled until she couldn't shuffle anymore.

Out of habit, she fanned a spread of cards but quickly snatched them up, deciding on an old-fashioned cut instead. Either way, the truth was going to come out. It always did.

Queenie nodded toward Chloe. "You're going to cut the deck three times. Be sure and use your left hand, the one closest to your heart."

"Okay," Chloe replied, as she made the first cut.

PAGE OF SWORDS
REVERSED

Queenie muttered "Unexpected events".

Chloe chewed on what little was left of the purple polish on her index finger. "Sometimes unexpected events are good, aren't they?"

Queenie didn't answer, motioning for Chloe to cut again.

With a trembling hand, Chloe made the second cut.

KNIGHT OF PENACLES
REVERSED.

Queenie uttered, "Carelessness. Not good."

Chloe spit a sliver of purple polish out of her mouth and into her hand. "So what... everybody is sometimes, aren't they?"

Queenie didn't utter a word as she moved what was left of the deck toward Chloe for the third and final cut.

Chloe turned the card face-up and there it was, just as Queenie knew it would be:

13th card of the MAJOR ARCANA
REVERSED

"Death," Queenie whispered.

Chloe screamed, jumped up from the table and ran for the car, kicking the dead porch bird with all her might, unaware that Queenie was already placing a fat black candle in the middle of the table.

10

Margaret wondered what Paul and her friends would say if they knew she was standing under a scraggly tree in front of a rundown shotgun house out in the middle of nowhere. All she needed was for some alligator to trundle out of the bayou. That way, at least, she'd have a great tale for everyone during cocktails at one of Paul's company's functions.

As the sun glistened overhead, Margaret's thoughts about Chloe and her beautiful baby, took her mind to places she didn't want to go.

Margaret willed herself to quit thinking about a pink and cream-colored nursery in one of their guest rooms, but it was hard.

Using only the tip of a gel nail, Margaret swished dust from out of the elaborate tapestry magnolia on one of her Louboutins.

With each swipe of her hand, the dust rose, then settled down on the velvety beige petals again. Margaret sighed. Another ruined pair of gorgeousness. Well, at least it wouldn't be a total loss since Zelda, her maid, wore the same size... or "close enough" as Zelda often said. Luckily, the maid didn't seem to care if Margaret's hand-me-downs weren't always perfect.

Margaret had just switched to wiping the other shoe when a scream from inside the house pierced the humid air.

Margaret swiveled toward the half-open screen door as Chloe burst through the shadowy darkness, kicking the dead bird in Margaret's direction.

Like a boomerang, the bird hit the porch railing and flew back.

With its claws open and beady eyes fixed in a deadly stare, the bird landed in Chloe's hair.

Unfortunately, the more Chloe swatted at the bird, the deeper its tiny claws became entangled.

As Margaret ran to help Chloe, she could barely make out the young girl's frantic words, "Help! Help! Get it... get it out! Please... get it away from me. Please!"

Margaret separated thin strands of Chloe's hair, trying not to touch the bird.

Margaret prayed the crow would fall out on its own but it stayed clinched in place until a fat brown hand slid effortlessly into the waves of Chloe's hair and gently pulled the creature out.

"Shush now, girl," Queenie said as she gave Chloe a pat on her head where the bird had been.

Free from the clutches of the dead bird, Chloe's shrieks softened to a sing-song wail as Queenie carried the dead bird to the side of her house and placed it beneath the top of a large sunflower that lay broken on the ground.

After dusting her hands together, Queenie pointed at Chloe. "I said hush and I mean it. No time for crying, child. I 'spect there's things to be settled and goodbyes to be said."

Chloe didn't answer but her soft moaning rose once again as she opened the back door of Margaret's Mercedes and dove in, barely missing hitting her head on MacKenzie's empty car seat.

***

Paul knew something wasn't right. If Margaret was going to be even a few minutes late, she always made sure her whereabouts were known, if not to Paul, then to someone in her family. *Where was she?*

He pulled his cell phone out of his pocket and swiped his index finger, moving through the names of clients, friends and family members until he found several numbers for Margaret's mom. No use calling the house. She was usually out shopping, at a spa or spearheading some charity benefit.

After dialing the first few numbers of her cell phone, Paul changed his mind and hit cancel. No need to worry anyone. At least, not yet. Hopefully, not at all.

According to the news, Gabby left a trail of destruction that would take days, maybe months to work through. More than likely, power wasn't back on in all the small towns between Baton Rouge and Houston and cell providers were still working to reinstate service.

Until he heard from Margaret, he didn't really want to involve others.

What if Margaret had absentmindedly turned toward NOLA or taken a wrong turn and had found herself on the way to Dallas instead of Houston? It could take her awhile to figure out how to get back and she might be determined to do it on her own instead of phoning him.

Margaret loved stopping in off-beat antique stores whenever she had a chance and she might have stopped along the way.

Margaret's delay could be due to any number of things.

Thrown into the mix was the "whole-woman-thing" Paul hadn't quite figured out yet: forgetfulness... hormones... mental fatigue. After so many miscarriages and fertility treatments, Margaret's emotions must be all over the place.

Paul bit his bottom lip and made note of the time. He'd wait until he heard from her even though that would be hard to do.

He missed his wife and wanted her home.

The sooner, the better.

***

Chloe's jagged sobs propelled Margaret into action. They were leaving.

One thing for sure, Margaret wasn't going on to Lake Charles until she had her hands on that precious baby even if she had to kick dead birds from here-to-there to get back inside the Psychic Queen of the Bayou's house to retrieve the little angel — which she did.

11

Ralph LeBlanc awoke with a start. It took him a second or two to realize the barking dog in his dream was in reality the unrelenting and annoying bark of his neighbor's Jack Russell.

Sunlight was peeking through the slats of the old Venetian blinds and the digital clock flashed 7:30.

It was rare for him to sleep past 6:30, even on weekends. By now, he was usually hidden behind the sports section of the Lake Charles Daily with a cup of strong Louisiana coffee in his hand before his wife Estelle shuffled to the kitchen to make breakfast for him and Tony.

Ralph wanted to turn off the sunlight and bury his head under his pillow but the guys at the station would wonder why their fearless leader hadn't made it in yet.

Ralph doubted anyone would be brave enough to phone him to inquire about his whereabouts but they'd probably crack a few jokes when he did show up.

To this day, Ralph was still amazed that he'd risen from the lower ranks to become a sheriff. He knew in his heart, he'd made some mistakes along the way, but all that was behind him now. It was best to just accept this lucky break and enjoy his good fortune.

It was no wonder he'd slept in, it was well after two in the morning before he heard the slam of Tony's car door and the squeak of a screen door.

Ralph never slept when Tony was out. Probably because he'd lifted too many broken bodies out of too many mangled cars.

The aroma of cinnamon rolls got him to the kitchen table more than the sound of his wife's voice when Estelle shouted up the stairs, "Ralph, you planning on staying in bed all day?"

The smell of sugar and cinnamon somewhat covered that of stale whiskey escaping from the upstairs bathroom where Tony was vomiting... again.

Ralph knew Tony had a fascination with liquor – the strong stuff, along with the women at the *Du-Drop Inn* on LaSalle Street.

Ralph had made it known to the Inn's owner Dan Steer that under no circumstances was alcohol to be served to Tony, or to any minor, for that matter.

Unfortunately, he also knew Tony wasn't above lifting a bottle of whiskey when the owner or some bartender was looking the other way.

In fact, Ralph had recently confiscated store security film that showed Tony swiping a bottle on a stroll through the local liquor store.

It was incredible what people would overlook for the son of the local sheriff.

In a way, Ralph thought it made it a little too easy for Tony to get by with murder.

After a couple of flushes of the upstairs toilet, Tony finally staggered to the kitchen. "Mom, I feel awful. Guess I'll skip school today and try to get some rest before baseball practice." He waved away the cinnamon roll Estelle brought toward him and mumbled, "Got anything to settle my stomach?"

Ralph watched Estelle reach for a bottle of anti-acids.

After shaking out a couple for Tony, she put her hand on his forehead. "You don't feel hot, baby, but then again, I don't want you spreading germs around if you're sick. It's barely been a week since you missed a couple of days with the flu. Hope you're not having a relapse."

Ralph wanted to laugh. He wondered if Estelle was really blind to Tony's carousing and drinking, or if she just chose to act as if she knew nothing. Either way, Tony had Stellie Beaudreau LeBlanc wrapped around his little finger.

Ralph had made it clear to Tony he was onto him and his shenanigans. Of course, Tony didn't seem to worry much about that, probably because his mom was the one with all the money.

As Ralph climbed the stairs, Estelle put the anti-acids back on the shelf. "I'll leave some money on the kitchen table in case you decide to go out later, Tony."

"Bless the Beaudreau oil fields!" Tony said with a laugh as he kissed his mom and left the table.

***

Estelle munched on a cinnamon roll, listening as Ralph started his shower and Tony hummed *Pennies, Pennies from Heaven*.

It was probably a good thing Tony didn't know the Beaudreau money wasn't near as much as it was before Estelle bought Ralph his sheriff job.

Estelle swirled the coffee in the bottom of her cup, remembering the twenty-two years she kept hoping and praying that Ralph would get the sheriff job on his own merit. She waited until it became apparent that wasn't going to happen before she resorted to making a few discreet phone calls.

A couple of weeks later, Ralph came home early on a Friday afternoon and joyously announced "I guess all of my hard work paid off. Get on your dancing shoes, Stellie, the new *Sheriff of Lake Charles* wants to take his wife out to dinner."

When Ralph announced his good news, her eyes had become misty as he twirled her around the living room. That part wasn't hard because it took considerably more money than she had anticipated.

Estelle smiled. Even so, her performance that evening was worthy of an Academy Award. First, a surprised look of shock followed by a smile of sheer pride and joy. Estelle practically laughed out loud just thinking about it.

After she swished the last of the lukewarm coffee down her throat, she smiled, saying, "And the award goes to Estelle Beaudreau LeBlanc of Good Old Lake Charles, Louisiana!"

After tearing off some foil to wrap up what was left of the cinnamon rolls, she stood at the sink watching the birds outside at the feeder.

Estelle wiped the counter free of crumbs while reaching for the phone to call her daughter Janie and confirm plans for lunch and a manicure later that day.

As she listened to the distant ring in her receiver, she muttered "Oh, well, Ralph's promotion was worth every penny" just as Janie answered.

Estelle was relieved to know that the phones were up and running after all the havoc of Gabby. Not being able to talk with Janie for the past two days had been worrisome.

Estelle knew and respected the value of family. In fact, it was through her own family connections that Estelle was privy to how politics worked all the way from the capital in Baton Rouge to the boardrooms in Shreveport.

It was simple really. Estelle could sum it up in two words: money talks and she had made hers talk, loud and clear.

As Janie's "Hello, Mom" filled the air, Estelle smiled and patted her hair, knowing no one would ever guess that she, a plump, middle-aged woman with mousy brown hair could get the job done. But she did. The shiny badge laying on the kitchen counter was proof.

Ralph was sheriff and that was that.

12

Ralph looped his belt around his waist. Then he automatically ran his hand across the handle of his pistol. He lifted his hat from the rack and shoved it down firmly on his thin balding hair.

He grabbed his badge from the counter and one last cinnamon bun from under some foil on a plate.

After blowing a kiss toward Estelle, he yelled a greeting to Janie in the general direction of the phone as he headed out in the glaring sunlight.

He wondered if he should talk to Dan Steer again about keeping Tony on the straight-and-narrow with more force than last time.

Maybe later. He was already running late.

***

After retrieving MacKenzie from the girl Kizzy, along with the baby bottle, Margaret now found herself driving down the rutted road once again.

Thankfully, the three of them were going away from the strange voodoo woman and ominous dead bird.

Chloe was laying in the backseat, still boo-hooing. However, baby MacKenzie seemed blissfully unaware and was snuggled safely in her car seat.

Occasionally, Margaret would get a glimpse of the baby's soft-curved chin in her rearview mirror.

Eventually, Chloe's crying stopped and she hopped over the seat back to the passenger side of the car. "Mind if I turn on the radio?"

Margaret nodded. "Sure."

"What kind of music do you like? I bet you don't like rock. Am I right?"

"If you really want to know I like classical music," Margaret answered softly.

"What do you mean classical music? Name something."

"Clair de Lune by Debussy, for example, or just about anything by Rachmaninoff."

Chloe rolled her eyes. "Well, do you care what kind of music we listen to right now?"

"Anything that comes in clear out here in the country is fine with me."

Chloe pushed buttons and ran the dial up and down the spectrum of satellite stations until the faint sound of hip-hop burst out between Gabby commentators.

Two minutes later, or so it seemed to Margaret, Chloe was at it again, trying to find something else on the radio.

Finally, the girl's fingers landed on a station playing remakes of old tunes such as "Stand by Me" and "Any Day Now". The artist were new and the renditions were different but the words were the same. Eventually, both Margaret and Chloe were singing along to most of them.

At the end of a song about a father who didn't have enough time to spend with his son, Chloe asked, "Kids?"

"You're not one to mince words, are you?" Margaret adjusted the driver's seat to give herself time to formulate what she wanted this cheeky kid to know.

As Margaret searched for the right words, she felt her jaw muscle tighten. Paul wasn't there to defend or protect her. Just what he needed to defend or protect her from, she didn't know exactly. Was it her imagined lack of womanhood, her own betraying older body, or just sheer bad luck?

"I asked if you had any kids. Well, do you?" Chloe asked again.

"No." Margaret sighed, realizing Chloe had been studying her face intently for several minutes. Their eyes locked and for some unexplainable reason, Margaret found herself pouring out her inner feelings about doctors, infertility, endometriosis, and teaching other people's children all the while clinging to hopes of having her own one day.

Margaret talked about the doctor who shook his head sadly and about Paul sending for adoption papers, and how they both avoided birthday parties for the children of their friends, sending lavish gifts instead, along with a somewhat plausible excuse for their absence.

Eventually, Margaret's voice dwindled to silence. She felt exhausted after releasing twelve years of frustration and immediately felt embarrassed at sharing so much of her soul... and to a stranger, at that.

She, Margaret, an intensely quiet and reserved person had spilled her guts to a complete stranger. She couldn't imagine what had made her do something so totally out of character.

Instead of looking sympathetic, Chloe took a deep breath and began to talk about the shock and embarrassment of finding herself pregnant by Tony LeBlanc, captain of the high school football team and star baseball player, who upon learning the results of Chloe's home pregnancy test, pleaded with her to have an abortion. He didn't want to take a chance on ruining things for himself or for his sister Janie's husband who was running for governor in the next election.

Margaret listened, making no comments.

As they neared the entrance ramp for I-10, Chloe talked about her feelings of being noticed by someone popular for the first time and then the total devastation of being dumped by the same hometown "hero". She talked about her life without a father and what it was like growing up the child of a single mother on welfare. She talked about her life on the "wrong side of the tracks" and her own determination to do better for her baby, the one in the faded pink baby dress banging a rattle against the window of Margaret's car.

Throughout her emotional un-burdening, Chloe toyed with a small silver heart that dangled from a delicate silver necklace chain.

When Margaret asked about it, Chloe looked at Margaret for several minutes. "It was my Mama's" she answered before laying

77

her head against the passenger window where she appeared to fall fast asleep.

The now sleeping Chloe took Margaret by surprise. Margaret wondered what kind of a person falls asleep traveling in the car of a complete stranger with a baby in the back seat.

A voice in her head whispered, "A very innocent or a very trusting one".

Margaret knew Chloe didn't fit into the first category, so she decided she must be trusting.

Margaret reached over and gently, motherly, brushed long strands of dark hair out of Chloe's lightly freckled face.

Instinctively, Margaret knew neither Chloe nor MacKenzie stood much of a chance. Their life would no doubt be one of financial worries and strife – at best.

How could one hope to escape the poverty and ignorance that was often bred in the rural swampland that began and ended in the warm waters of the Gulf of Mexico?

13

Paul tapped the ignition button on the company van and guided it out of the dimly lit parking garage. He knew the five junior architects who piled in the van with him were most likely in awe of him. One had even called him "the wonder boy" to his face.

A few tried to attach themselves to Paul in a professional way.

Paul was always kind to the newbies but the truth was, Paul was totally focused on his job and not a lot on the personalities involved.

The six of them headed out past the refineries to the job site on the east side of town.

They passed the San Jacinto Monument and laughed about the pungent odor that was always present when smoke billowed skyward from the refineries, which was pretty much all of the time.

Paul smiled thinking of Margaret's recycling efforts. Just last week, he had hauled a recycling bin full of newspapers and magazines to the street. Peeking out from under a pile of sports magazines was an old Baby Time.

At one time, Margaret subscribed to several parenting magazines but over the years she'd let the subscriptions expire. Paul guessed it was an embarrassment for Margaret to have the mailman deliver the same magazines year-after-year and never spot any signs of a baby or child. No stroller was ever parked askew on the porch, no infant seat visible in the back of Margaret's car, nor even so much as a toy dropped carelessly in the yard.

Margaret's silent suffering tugged at his heart and strengthened the deep love he felt for her. He thought about how surprised the five younger guys riding along would be if they knew how much of a failure the "wonder boy" felt inside.

As the group reached their destination, Paul's Berluti shoe hit the brake harder than he intended.

Everyone laughed as they tumbled out of the van in a flash of perfectly creased shirts and slacks. After running a hand through his professionally styled hair, Paul glanced at his Rolex. Perfect timing. Of course.

Not only did Jackson, Burke & Connelly believe their employees should be paid well, they expected them to be on time.

Whenever the firm was mentioned around the southern part of the United States, one could practically hear a sigh of envy among other architects and engineers. The proof of it was in the volume of carefully filled-out resumes that arrived there daily.

Of course, only the brightest and best would be chosen for an interview.

14

Back on I-10, Margaret returned her attention to the increasing amount of traffic.

Whenever there was a decent space between her car and others around her, her mind went to the spare bedroom right across the hall from her master bedroom. The proximity would ensure that either she or Paul would hear the softest cry or whimper. The window seat would add charm filled with pastel pillows and cute stuffed animals.

As Margaret's car rolled along, she found herself humming songs from her own fairytale childhood.

Of course, adoption was an option, but for Margaret, adoption had always represented giving-in and admitting she would never give birth. To her, it would be like "throwing in the towel".

However, recently the babies in her dreams didn't look like Paul's baby pictures, nor her own, for that matter.

Paul seemed fine with the idea of adopting a child. His own mother had been adopted as a child.

Paul often teased her affectionately about her abundance of pride. The last time they'd had a serious baby discussion, he'd gone a bit further when he suggested that her pride might eventually keep Margaret from getting what she wanted most in the world.

At the time, Margaret brushed off his words because she was sure she would eventually get pregnant and they would have a good laugh at all they'd gone through. That never happened.

Margaret found it hard to admit that months of not conceiving had turned into years. Sadly, it seemed like Paul's prediction would be right after all.

In the past, things had always come easily for Margaret. She was the baby in her family, the youngest of four – all girls.

From the moment she was born, her family had catered to her every whim. It was a favorite story in the family that when Paul asked Margaret's dad for her hand in marriage, her father told him that he and

Margaret's mother had tended to spoil Margaret a bit since she was the baby of the family.

Paul passed the test because his reply was that he intended to "keep up the tradition". He had.

Margaret wasn't a scholar although she made good grades. She'd learned long ago to "play the game" of looking interested in every word her professors uttered.

She was never tardy and turned in her assignments on time. All of that, along with her kilowatt smile never failed to push C's to B's and B's to A's.

After graduating from LSU, she and Paul packed up their belongings and headed to Houston where Paul had a job waiting for him.

A month later, Margaret was hired as a classroom elementary teacher with very little effort while her friends were still job hunting or signing up to substitute in hopes of getting a "foot in the door".

It wasn't that Margaret was aggressive. Things just seemed to fall into place for her. Whenever she thought about it, she attributed it to her deep belief in God and basically, the goodness of people.

Margaret had accomplished everything she wanted to accomplish, except the thing that mattered the most to her – to have a baby.

Every so often, Margaret glanced over at Chloe and back at MacKenzie as the car clicked off the miles.

As Margaret steered the car down the exit ramp at Lake Charles, Chloe was instantly awake, leaving Margaret to wonder if Chloe had only been pretending to be asleep. Maybe Chloe had been lost in her own thoughts like Margaret herself had been for the past several miles.

Strangely, Chloe's first words were "You seem really rich, but I need to know for sure".

Margaret sucked in her breath. "I guess. Of course, there's always going to be those with more and those with less in the world."

"I mean can you afford a lifetime of providing for someone else?" Chloe swiped a few strands of hair from her face. "Hey, turn here and stay straight until we get to Mead Road. Then, pull in at the gas station on the corner."

Margaret gave a show of closely watching the street signs and pulled in to the lot of the gas station before turning off the motor.

Chloe jumped out and opened the back door to retrieve MacKenzie.

Margaret turned to face Chloe. "Yes."

Chloe looked at Margaret for several long minutes like she had something more to say. Once she opened her mouth but closed it again. Instead, she thanked Margaret for the ride and then turned abruptly to yell and wave to a young guy half-hidden behind tools, old car parts, and a spark plug display.

Margaret watched Chloe straighten her thin shoulders and wrap her arms tightly around MacKenzie as she moved away from the car and Margaret.

Margaret's attention shifted to the young guy, probably Chloe's friend Eddie.

Margaret knew for sure this youngster was no local football player. He reminded her of a best friend years ago in high school who was a really nice guy, but one many girls would pass over looking for "Mr. Big Man on Campus", only to realize years later they'd passed up a real gem.

As the guy reached to take MacKenzie from Chloe, he protectively wrapped his other arm around Chloe.

If Margaret had to guess, she'd bet that Chloe's future would probably begin-and-end with this auto mechanic. Their's would be a life surrounded by rubble, mounds of old car parts and the smell of oil and grease. No doubt, it'd be a life of living paycheck-to-paycheck with the constant worry of where their next meal might come from at various stages along the way. On the other hand, it would be a life full of kisses, hugs and more delightful chubby babies.

Margaret felt a pang of envy for the two who had so little but yet, so very much. Yes, it would be a rich life, but not the kind that could be totaled in dollars and cents.

15

Estelle backed her white Cadillac out of the carport and down the bumpy road. Immediately, she noticed that the red needle on her gas tank pointed to low. She was glad that Tony was out-of-her-reach. She could have hauled off and smacked him one.

Tony knew the stipulation for borrowing her car was to return it with a full tank of gas. Of course, he never did. "Idle promises" she said aloud.

Feeling depressed, she headed for Bill Buckley's gas station.

As she drove, she thought about the differences between her son and daughter. Janie had always been "every mother's dream child". Estelle often told others that Janie was her friend first and her daughter second. And she was.

On the other hand, she and Ralph had grown accustomed to being summoned by a distraught teacher or impatient principal eager to suspend Tony for one infraction or another.

Both of them had talked to the kid until they were "blue in the face" but it seemed like there was always something new to worry about where Tony was involved.

After two stop signs and one red light, Estelle arrived at the station where she was greeted cheerfully by Mr. Buckley's employee Eddie Smith, a classmate of Tony's.

"Looks like it's going to be another nice day, Mrs. LeBlanc." Eddie shut her hood with a click after checking the oil.

"Yes, I just love the weather in the south, don't you Eddie?"

Eddie smiled. "Sure do".

"Oh, I want to pick up a Times Picayune while I'm here. I want to see what's on sale over at the mall in New Orleans."

Eddie picked up a paper from a stack with others. "Here you go, Mrs. LeBlanc. Hope you find some bargains."

"Well, I don't know if I'll make it all the way to New Orleans this weekend or not, but I would like to take Janie on a shopping spree and I could use an outing, too."

Eddie smiled. "Well, be sure and tell Tony hello for me."

Estelle nodded as she replaced her charge card in her wallet and noticed for the first time, a slim girl standing in the shadowy doorway to the rear of the station. In her arms was a baby that looked exactly like Tony at that age. So much so, Estelle stopped dead in her tracks.

As if a buzzer had gone off or an alarm had sounded, the girl shifted the baby in her arms and scurried back through the doorway back into the shadows.

Estelle instinctively took two steps in the direction of the doorway but after several long moments, jammed her wallet in her purse and retreated to the plush leather safety of her car.

***

Chloe stood still.

Listening.

Waiting.

It wasn't until she heard the door of Cadillac that she could safely let herself breathe.

Hopefully, the danger of the truth being discovered by Estelle LeBlanc was more imagined than real.

91

Chloe reassured herself if Estelle LeBlanc guessed she'd just come face-to-face with the heir to the Beaudreau fortune, she wouldn't have driven off.

If there was one thing Chloe possessed, it was "street smarts". She knew that once the LeBlanc family thought through the ramifications of the mother-of-their-grandchild claiming the child's share to the oil fortune, she'd probably have to hand over MacKenzie to Tony and his family to raise. They were smart people and the type who would hire lawyers to fight to get the baby. Heck, she bet they'd even twist the law to suit their needs.

Giving MacKenzie to Tony was the only thing she would never willingly do. He didn't deserve a second chance. He'd had his chance the day she told him about her pregnancy. She'd go hungry before she took one thin dime from them for herself... or MacKenzie, but she doubted any of them would believe it.

Probably no judge would either.

16

Estelle's mind was racing a mile a minute. Surely, the unknown girl could not be the mother of Tony's baby. Estelle would know, wouldn't she? She could read Tony like an open book and he didn't seem any different than the usual carefree kid he'd always been. He certainly didn't act like he was hiding some big secret. Still, there was no denying the strong similarity of the baby to Tony when he was that age.

Estelle usually chose to ignore what she didn't want to see, but for a moment, she thought maybe she should call Ralph and have this girl questioned until they knew the truth. This is what paternity tests were for, wasn't it?

In the end, Estelle gave the gas station one last look in her rear mirror and decided that it was in the best interest of Janie's husband's political career to keep driving. Any kind of small town scandal could cost the family dearly.

Estelle had already made sure that her son-in-law was a major contender in the race for governor and that had significantly lowered her already dwindling bank account once again.

Estelle said to the Times Picayune in the seat beside her, "It's a good thing Daddy isn't alive to see how fast my inheritance is slipping away."

Ralph would hit the ceiling if he knew that it was Estelle who had provided the private room in the New Orleans' Super Dome, complete with elevator access and a catered meal every time the Saints played instead of Janie's husband. Estelle knew those little perks kept Janie's husband from roaming like he had in the beginning and it was probably going to cost her more to keep his girlfriends from telling their story when he declared his intention of running for office.

Estelle pushed the mental picture of the baby in the gas station out of her mind. She simply couldn't afford to give it, the girl, or Eddie another thought.

"Ignorance is bliss!" she stated to the paper, and her purse in the passenger seat. With that final utterance, she pushed her pointed black leather shoe harder on the gas petal and zoomed toward the bridge that would carry her to the other side of Lake Charles and the comfort of Janie's face.

Not in her wildest imagination would Estelle ever divulge her suspicions to Janie, or to anyone for that matter. She had learned a long time ago, in the words of her own mother, to keep her mouth shut. Her family, the Beaudreau family wasn't a loving or affectionate family unless an "outsider" threatened their wealth or position in society. Only then, did they band together. But band together they did.

Yes, the Beaudreau family always kept their affairs and family business private and Estelle would do just that. Just to be sure, she needed to make sure she had enough money – always, and made a mental note to call about sending some equipment to punch a few more holes on some family land.

It would be costly but it wouldn't hurt to drill a new well or two.

17

The heat wasn't anywhere near where it would be later in the summer. Still, the humid air hit Paul like a furnace the moment he and the others left the van and made their way down a newly constructed sidewalk of old Chicago brick. It was brick made by hand that Paul had specified less than a year ago.

A couple of construction workers were still in the process of staining the wooden walking bridge that crossed over a small man-made pond.

Paul smiled, knowing soon the movement of the exotic fish against lush landscaping would provide the perfect ambiance he intended for the building to project.

He glanced at the younger architects with him. Would any of them be able to give even the smallest detail of a project this size the amount of attention it deserved? He had high hopes that they could.

Paul pulled his cell out of his pocket and glanced to see if he had missed a call from Margaret but there was nothing. Unfortunately, the project manager was greeting them before he had time to check his email and texts.

Even in his worried state of mind, Paul knew he had to give all of his attention to a variety of little things that still needed to be checked off the punch list.

***

While waiting for the light to change, Margaret tried to find a classical station on the radio. Mostly, she found either static or hurricane damage updates.

Once the light changed, Margaret swung back on I-10.

As Margaret started down the bridge on the west side of Lakes Charles, she looked with familiarity and fascination at the numerous miniature replicas of pistols that formed the ironwork railing of the old bridge. She wondered if the visual show of guns was meant to be a symbol of strength, or a sign of surrender.

Every couple, like a city, has their own history. Maybe even more importantly, they hold their own destiny. Margaret couldn't help but wonder if she should surrender her own desires to have a baby for the good of their family – Paul and herself. Even if there were only two of them, she and Paul were a family. Paul once said "There's no certain number of people that make a family".

"You're my family, Paul," Margaret had replied.

"And you're mine," Paul had answered with a kiss.

Margaret accepted Paul's definition of a family outwardly but inwardly she knew they'd feel more like a family once there was a child to love and bond them together even more.

Margaret descended to the bottom of the bridge and looked down the road that shot straight for Texas. The brightness of the sun caused her to look around for her sunglasses. Instead of her Dolce and Gabbana glasses, she spied the tattered car seat. MacKenzie's car seat.

"What kind of a person is so careless that they'd leave their baby's car seat in the car of a stranger?" Margaret said aloud.

Gently, but forcefully, the answer came. *The kind of a person who wants to be found again.*

Margaret eased her car to the side of the road. Before making a U-turn, she looked carefully both ways... and deep in her heart.

18

On the other side of the bridge, Eddie watched Chloe from behind a display of energy drinks on the counter. She seemed unaware of him as her eyes searched the horizon. MacKenzie was asleep on a blanket in the station's backroom and the quiet was deafening.

When the last customer left and no one appeared on the horizon, Chloe bit her lip. "If you don't need me to go with you to get my car, can I borrow yours? I'm tired and I want to go home."

Eddie doubted there was much to eat in Chloe's trailer. "I tell you what... I'll take the tow truck back for your car later this evening. Don't leave yet. Buckley's gone for the day and I've got some gumbo cooking on a hot plate in the back and no one to share it with."

Chloe gave the highway one last look before nodding okay.

Eddie smiled. "Missed your company Chloe-girl."

"Me, too." Chloe mumbled before disappearing from the front of the gas station.

Eddie grabbed a package of unopened plastic bowls from a shelf and followed Chloe with MacKenzie in his arms.

They were his family. They had to be because neither he, Chloe or MacKenzie had anyone else.

***

Margaret fumbled for the emergency flashers that she had never used before now.

As she swung her car around, she said to the bridge looming ahead, "I dare any policeman to stop me… after all, isn't a life-changing situation considered an emergency? Well, this is going to be a life-changing situation. I can just feel it!"

Margaret raced back toward the bridge with the little steel guns, back toward the gas station with a mechanic named Eddie and back toward her future in a faded pink baby dress.

It was the race of her life and she knew it.

Of course, she could be dead wrong. Only time would tell.

19

Sheriff LeBlanc wiped his forehead as the sun grew higher. He could have been sitting in his soft leather chair down at the station but the familiarity of watching and waiting for a speeding car made him feel more important than pushing papers around on his desk.

He checked his watch and figured he'd only stay ten more minutes, or so, until he was sure that Sue Liberman had switched over from breakfast items to the lunch menu at *Café Charles* and then he'd head on over and order the daily special which usually consisted of some kind of meat along with lumpy mashed potatoes and canned green beans.

Even if the food was lacking at *Café Charles*, it was the one place left in Lake Charles where every face was a familiar one.

For the most part, everyone who ate there had grown up eating together in school cafeterias and then later at various functions such as potluck dinners after church or holiday picnics in the park.

"Old Lake Charles" knew Sue's was the place to get your curiosity filled along with your belly.

Years ago, Estelle had said "If Sue would put as much effort into her cooking as she does keeping up with everyone and everything, we'd have us a first-class restaurant".

Feeling argumentative that day, Ralph replied, "The food just wouldn't taste the same without a few morsels of gossip, now would it Stellie?"

"Maybe not, but Sue needn't think she can pretend to be the friend of good Christian women just to get gossip to serve her customers along with greasy food. In fact, she told several of us that she was planning on joining our Sunday School class. Can you imagine? Any time a prayer request went out, it would be all over town!"

"And just what's wrong with that?"

"Our class, the *Christian Converts*, is tight and we confide in each other but we don't want our business dished-out with a big spoonful of creamed onions!"

Ralph laughed. "Frankly, I'd tell the *Christian Converts* not to lose any sleep over it. I haven't heard her knocking at the church door, have you?"

Estelle spat out "Laugh all you want Ralph LeBlanc, but there's some that say food and gossip isn't all Sue's been serving the community".

Janie had spilled the beans years ago when she excitedly pointed out her dad's patrol car at Sue's house one night as Estelle drove her and Tony home from a school carnival.

Ralph had gone to great lengths to persuade her that Sue had called the station about a burglary but Estelle was never firmly convinced. It remained a sore spot between them but in the end, Estelle had chosen to ignore what may or may not have been.

Still, Estelle was always quick to point out, Sue's wasn't the only place to eat in Lake Charles.

As Ralph started to flip off his radar gun, the emergency flashers on a gold Mercedes caught his eye. The car made a U-turn and headed back toward the bridge. Ralph clocked the car at sixty-three in a forty-five.

Ralph turned on his siren and shot into action. His movements were swift and sure. He was behind the speeding car in a few short moments.

The driver of the gold Mercedes pulled to the side of the road.

Even though Ralph saw it was a woman and she appeared to be all alone in the car, he unfastened the leather strap that held his gun firmly at his side.

Ralph never approached a car without making sure the gun was within his quick grasp if needed. It was a habit from years of practice and training. As Ralph walked toward the car, his stomach growled. He sure hoped this wouldn't take long. He didn't want to miss the noonday crowd at Sue's.

Ralph drew closer to the car and made note of the Texas plates and a small discreet decal on the back window. Probably a parking decal from one of those high-end residential places with a gatehouse. Ralph chuckled. "Certainly not from around here."

A slim and gorgeous, beauty-queen kind of gal rolled down her window.

It took a minute for Ralph to regain his composure after the girl looked up at him with the bluest eyes he'd ever seen.

Although he could have gotten the information from the computer in his squad car, Ralph stated, "Need to see your driver's license... and your insurance papers."

"Sure thing, officer."

The bluest-eyes-ever turned away from him and slim manicured hands flipped through the glove compartment until Ralph was handed an insurance card.

From the corner of his eye, Ralph saw the lady glance at her diamond-encrusted watch.

Now, Ralph's curiosity was really piqued. Most of the women he stopped for speeding tried to cry their way out of a ticket. The rest tried to flirt their way out it.

This gal was different. Ralph felt like he was nothing more than a hindrance that was keeping her from a mission of some kind.

Well, this was going to cost her. Of course, from the look of things, she could afford to pay.

As Ralph wrote out her ticket, he couldn't help noticing her shiny hair and expensive casual clothes.

Even without her Houston address in his hand, Ralph would have known this was no ordinary Lake Charles housewife.

He briefly wondered if she was a model or movie star but quickly dismissed the idea because no one of any real importance would be traveling through this "neck of the world".

"Probably just some rich Houston gal gliding through life on her daddy's money... kinda like Estelle" Ralph thought as he handed the ticket through the open window and into the manicured hand.

Ralph walked away thinking the whole thing rather strange. Rich, yes. Gorgeous, yes. But apparently, not into her kid by the looks of that filthy-dirty, car seat in the back.

"Just goes to show, the rich are different," Ralph muttered in the humid Louisiana air.

20

Paul's office was cooler than usual. He pushed a button and asked his secretary if he'd had any calls while he was at the job site.

In a matter of seconds, his secretary entered his office with a stack of notes from various clients. None of the messages were from Margaret.

Paul picked up the phone and dialed his home phone number just in case Margaret had made it back to Houston already.

The house phone rang four times before the answering machine picked up his call. He punched in a couple of numbers and listened to the recording. There were a few calls on it but nothing of any importance. He hung up and called again to listen to the recording once again just to hear Margaret say "You've reached the

Sinclairs. We're not home right now, so leave a message please". He knew it was foolish but for some strange reason, he felt calmer. He hung up the phone and motioned for Don Jackson, a recent employee who was hovering in the doorway.

As Don entered his office, Paul turned his attention to the *Cowboys of Texas Museum* that would soon be under an extensive renovation.

Renovations were not Paul's favorite. Generally, more work and money was always involved than anyone anticipated at first.

However, shareholders were arriving in less than an hour and he and Don needed to polish the profit calculations before Paul gave another sales pitch in the conference room for the second time today.

To top it off, Paul's desk was stacked high with resumes of hopeful young men wanting to come on board at the firm. Paul knew he needed to line up some interviews for Friday but now wasn't the time. Glancing at his watch, he cleared his desk, and his mind. He needed to concentrate on every detail of the job.

As his secretary entered and handed both men a cold bottle of water, Paul circled a preliminary seven figure number on the last set of drawings.

Then, the two men talked about an upcoming charity golf tournament and

planned their strategy for the treacherous
thirteen hole.

21

Margaret inched her car into the lot of the gas station and peered nervously around. The place appeared empty and Margaret who had felt so excited and free-of-doubt a few minutes ago, now felt let-down and extremely disappointed. She'd missed her chance. The girl was gone. The baby, too.

Feeling unsure, she decided to at least try to find someone who would see that Chloe got the car seat back.

As she walked into the gas station, she was startled by the sound of bells that were tied to the door handle.

From behind a curtain a man called, "Be with you in a moment."

Margaret didn't have time to answer before the man swept through the doorway.

Margaret smiled. It was Eddie. "Your friend Chloe left her car seat in my car. I thought maybe you could give it to her."

Eddie smiled. "Why don't you give it to her, yourself? She and MacKenzie are still here."

Eddie motioned for Margaret to follow him into the back room. "Hungry?"

"I had breakfast in Baton Rouge and some candy on the way."

"Well, follow me. You're about to eat the best gumbo this side of the Mississippi River!"

Margaret laughed and so did Chloe who smiled slightly when Margaret handed the car seat to her.

Eddie wiped off an old Formica table and pulled out a chair for Margaret.

As Eddie hustled about, clanking dishes and silverware, he kept up a conversation with Margaret, asking about Houston and her life in general.

Margaret felt totally at home in the cramped corner of the garage as Eddie bustled around both her and Chloe.

A couple of times, Eddie even waited on a customer-or-two while Margaret and Chloe ate the gumbo.

Eddie was so charming, Margaret didn't mind his barrage of questions and felt like she was among old friends. Neither Chloe nor Eddie seemed intimidated by her gold watch, expensive clothes or the embarrassing large diamond in her wedding ring. They didn't even seem to notice. Their conversation showed more interest in Margaret, the person.

Margaret thought how much she'd like for Paul to meet them but then chuckled inwardly about how absurd all of this would sound to him.

Even to her, it felt unreal to be hunkered down, eating a thick, spicy soup in a gas station with two strangers. At the same time, it seemed perfectly normal.

Eddie put the last of the gumbo in a plastic container and into a large ice chest. "Margaret, Chloe tells me you're a teacher. What grade do you teach?"

"Fourth."

Chloe piped up, "I don't remember much about my teachers. Every time the rent came due we moved so it seemed like the minute I made a friend, I had to say goodbye and start all over again."

Margaret tried not to give Chloe the pity smile she was feeling. "That's too bad."

Chloe continued, "Teachers always seemed to hate it when I moved in and most were glad to see me go."

Eddie patted Chloe's shoulder. "Ah... I doubt it."

A feeling of sadness overwhelmed Margaret for the little girl Chloe must have

117

been. Margaret looked at MacKenzie and hoped history wouldn't repeat itself.

There was a lull in the conversation and Eddie turned on the radio. It claimed to be the only gospel station in Louisiana that played fifty-five minutes of music without a commercial.

One-by-one, all three of them began to sing along with one song after another. Margaret was surprised at the quality and range of Eddie's voice and the softness of Chloe's as they sung old familiar hymns from the past.

While going to the front to help a customer, Eddie had plopped MacKenzie in Margaret's lap and she gently rocked her in her arms as she sang.

Eventually, MacKenzie squirmed and Margaret pulled her to a sitting position and clapped MacKenzie's hands to the rhythm of the music. MacKenzie laughed and made delightful baby noises the entire time.

Margaret knew Paul would like Chloe and Eddie both very much but she knew it would be MacKenzie who would steal his heart.

Margaret made no move to leave the now familiar gas station on Mead Road, a hundred miles from Houston, until Chloe said, "I need to get home."

Margaret made a mental note that Chloe did not say that she and MacKenzie needed to go home or that she needed to get MacKenzie settled-in for a long afternoon nap. Was Chloe giving an answer to the question that had never been verbalized or was it just wishful thinking?

Margaret wondered if Chloe had purposefully let Eddie give MacKenzie to her to hold most of the afternoon while watching from the other side of the wobbly table or if it meant absolutely nothing.

At any rate, Margaret offered to drive Chloe home. So, Eddie said he'd go for Chloe's car.

***

After answering the third noise complaint in less than a month about the same barking dog, Ralph swung in Buckley's to fill-up.

Ralph was surprised to see the gold Mercedes with the Texas plates parked in the lot.

At first, he thought maybe he should see what was going on, but decided to cruise out of the lot and go to another station for gas, not that he would have minded another look at the stunning beauty, but his inner voice seemed to scream for him to stay away... for no reason.

***

Paul rolled up a couple of museum revisions and handed the blueprints to Don Jackson. "We'll zip-drive more over this week but be sure and tell them we can't produce the final drawings until they give us a budgeted amount. I'm not comfortable working with general estimates. Too much riding on a job of this scope."

"Thanks, Paul. I understand and if we weren't so pressed for time, I wouldn't ask you to do it this way."

Don nodded. He sure didn't want to ruin the relationship he had there with Paul but in the past year Don had worked at Jackson, Burke & Connelly, he'd never heard Paul sound so tense.

"Working with the best architectural firm in the south is like hitching your wagon to a star," Don had told his wife not more than a week ago when Paul landed the resort job in St. Croix.

Paul walked toward his office door with Don. "Hey man, sorry. I didn't mean to sound so gruff. I'm just edgy. My wife is traveling from her parent's home in Baton Rouge and I thought she'd he here by now."

"No problem. And if she's anything like my wife, she's lost track-of-time and is looking at knickknacks in some store along

120

the way. Besides, things are still a bit out of whack from Gabby. Your wife may be held up here-or-there along the way for emergency personal or utility trucks to cut away tree branches down on the highway. I'm sure she'll show up soon."

"You're right. Guess the bachelor life isn't the one for me," Paul laughed as they parted ways.

***

Estelle loved spending time with her daughter. Janie always had the most interesting and entertaining antidotes to tell her. It wasn't often that Janie had a day without her husband Archer, but when she did, she and Estelle often spent the day getting a manicure, pedicure or perhaps, a facial.

Today, Janie seemed content just to stay home which suited Estelle just fine.

Janie dished some local gossip which prompted Estelle to say *"Dit mon la verite!"* in her best imitation of a Cajun voice.

"You're right on that one... it is too unbelievable to be true, that's for sure," Janie replied.

"Oh, look... there's a *caimon* on the counter!" Estelle replied with a hearty laugh.

Through her own laugher, Janie said, "I don't see any alligator! Could it be that you're trying to distract me from the disaster which was once my orderly and clean kitchen? They should have named the hurricane *Archer* instead of *Gabby*!"

Estelle laughed. "Baby girl, are you sure you're ready to be the wife of a governor *when... not if...* Archer wins the election?"

"Truthfully mom, I always envisioned a quieter, less complicated life for the two of us. Who knew his political ambitions would carry him further than Lake Charles!"

Estelle rinsed a couple of dishes for the dishwasher before answering. "I'm not sure any of us did."

"I swear mom, there's no stopping him. Promise not to tell this but sometimes we drive all the way over to Baton Rouge so that he can stare at the Governor's mansion."

"My lips are sealed."

Janie closed a box of open cereal and put it in the walk-in pantry before continuing, "I do have to admit, the mansion is beautiful nestled under all those Magnolia trees. The lawn is beautifully manicured and the grass looks like velvet."

"I know. I've always thought it looks like a postcard when the Azaleas explode every April with those large fragrant blossoms of red, pink, purple and white. It really is lovely and would be a great place for you and Archer, as long as you come back to Lake Charles when his term is over."

"Of course we will, but mom, the inside is just as gorgeous, although we've only been invited there a time or two."

Estelle put the last of dirty dishes in the dishwasher and dropped in a pellet of detergent. She closed it and pushed the start button. "Janie, you'll be the prettiest First Lady this old bayou state has seen in a long time!"

"I don't know, mom. I know Archer wishes I was more educated and I wish I was more outgoing like Tony and Dad."

"You'll be fine. Quit worrying. Come on, let's go running around. A new dress is just the very thing to restore your confidence!"

It wasn't the outward things that worried Estelle about Janie stepping on a larger stage, it was the insecurities that Janie never seemed able to shake.

Estelle had done all that Beaudreau money could do. Janie had a million dollar smile after years of braces and her eyes were a vivid blue, thanks to colored-contact lenses. Estelle had provided every piece of exercise equipment on the market as well as a gym membership for life.

At the beginning of every season, the two of them flew to New York and made numerous trips to New Orleans for stylish clothes that couldn't be found in Lake Charles or Beaumont.

If only she could buy a heaping dose of self-confidence for her daughter, she would.

"You'll feel better if we get out a while. Go freshen up and let's head out," Estelle said, digging in her purse for a tube of lipstick.

With a bang of the backdoor against the wall, Tony burst in Janie's kitchen. "Hey, mom."

"Tony, what a surprise. I didn't expect to see you here today. I thought you weren't feeling well and had decided to stay in bed all day."

"I'm feeling better now. Can I borrow your car?"

"First, say hello to your sister."

"Hi, sis. Mom, can I have your car?"

Estelle glanced out the breakfast room windows. "How did you get here?"

"I hooked a ride with Patrolman Harris."

"Tony, you know your dad told you not to use the Lake Charles Police Department as your personal taxi service."

"Sorry, I forgot. Do I get the car or not?"

As she had many times in the past, Janie came to Tony's rescue. "Mom, I'll take you home after we run around. I want to stop at Burdette's Furniture over on Mead. There's a desk there that I've been thinking about buying for Archer."

Estelle ignored Tony for the moment. "Well, we need to make it a quick trip. I'm signed up to volunteer over at the hospital from four to six this afternoon. Guess you can drop me off there and Ralph can come for me later."

Tony planted a big kiss on Estelle's cheek. "Well, come on then. Hand me the keys!"

"Not so fast, young man. Tony, I'm warning you to be careful. I don't want a dent or scratch on my car. Don't forget our agreement... fill up the tank before bringing it home and don't be late. We're eating at 7:00 sharp." Estelle's words sounded harsh but they were delivered with a warm smile.

Tony planted another kiss on Estelle's cheek, grabbed the car keys, a bag of cookies from the pantry and bounded out the door.

Janie smiled. "That boy could charm a snake out of a tree."

"I'm not sure whether that's good or not." Estelle said as she watched her white Cadillac fly out of sight.

Estelle glanced at her watch. "Let's get going. I've got to watch the time."

Janie reached for her purse. "I'm proud of you mom. You've stayed at that volunteer job for longer than most people would have, that's for sure.

"It gets me out of the house and keeps me in the loop. Best place to find out what's going on in little old Lake Charles. Now, shake-a-tail-feather and let's go."

22

Ralph left the courthouse at three o'clock sharp. He felt good knowing another criminal was going to spend some time in jail. This was certainly a far better ending than some of the other trials he'd testified-in, only to have a bleeding heart jury or some judge set the jerk free.

Once back in the safety of his car, he let out a loud, long belch. That greasy food down at Sue's was going to be the death of him yet.

Ralph headed back toward the station thinking about Sue and the week they'd spent together two years ago in Galveston. He still couldn't believe how easy it had been to pull it off. Estelle fell "hook, line and sinker" for the *Weapons Training Week* alibi he created.

There were probably people around town who knew about his affair with Sue but thankfully, they kept their mouths shut.

127

Ralph didn't worry about Estelle finding out because everyone had a high regard for her. He couldn't think of a soul who would want to hurt her. After all, it was always Estelle who was first with a casserole for a new mom or the one to place flowers on the grave of a friend long after even the family had stopped going to the cemetery.

The Beaudreau money would have been worth marrying her for even if she hadn't turned out to be a good wife and companion. Not a hot sexy one, just a good one.

Ralph couldn't help thinking back about the smell of Sue that summer as they walked with their arms wrapped around each other across the warm sand to the music of the crashing waves. It was romantic and it was exciting, probably because it was forbidden.

Ralph knew that Sue would jump at the chance for another fling but for some unknown reason, he just didn't feel inclined to repeat what he knew was a mistake in the first place.

It was enough to see her over at the diner almost every day.

As Ralph swung into his reserved parking space at the station, he immediately spotted Tony sitting on the hood of Jimmy Harris's patrol car. He was surprised that Estelle had given Tony her car again for the second day in a row but there was no mistaking the pearly white Cadillac parked in the lot.

Tony hopped off the patrol car before Ralph shoved his gear in park but Ralph emerged yelling anyway. "Get off that car... now!"

"I'm sorry, dad. I wasn't thinking!"

"That's the trouble, Tony, you're never thinking!"

"Hey dad, I need to borrow some money. I'll pay you back, I promise."

Tony ended his plea with a smile that Ralph knew made the girls weak. Otherwise, why would Tony get away with the things he did where the ladies were concerned?

After much grumbling, Ralph handed Tony a twenty dollar bill along with a strong warning that he'd better get a part-time job or he was on his way to work for Ralph's brother on an off-shore rig south of Morgan City.

Tony slipped the money in his wallet without so-much as a thank-you.

"Your days of sleeping late, skipping class, and only showing up for baseball practice are coming to an end."

"But dad, you don't mean that. I've got the state championship coming up. Not my fault that the hurricane flooded Cameron Parish, causing school closures, which has caused a severe lack of time for ball practice!"

"Off-shore, kid, off-shore."

"Whatever you say."

Tony jumped in the Cadillac and spun out of the lot. If only he could convince his mom to buy something sporty instead of this beast of a car!

Thinking about baseball led him to thinking about a certain cheerleader. She vaguely reminded him of Chloe... and okay, yes, a dozen other girls he had courted ardently during the past year. All of whom were eager to be the girlfriend of the good-looking, dimpled, and extremely popular quarterback and possible pitcher of the State Champions.

No, Tony felt no qualms taking advantage of his good fortune but he'd do all that he had to do to stay away from Morgan City or any off-shore rig. The action was here in Lake Charles. If anything, he planned to branch out to bigger playgrounds after graduation. Maybe New Orleans or Houston. An apartment in Dallas was in the running, too.

Tony was glad that Chloe's "Little Problem" hadn't created the sensation that it could have caused. He was grateful that the girl had kept quiet. It was funny, he couldn't remember a lot about her except she had soft hair and a sweet voice. There were times he wondered if the baby was a boy or a girl, but decided he didn't want to know badly enough to risk stirring up a potential problem, although he wouldn't mind being with the girl again.

It was a wonder his dad let him get away without marrying the girl. That, in itself, still amazed him. Probably because Tony had the goods on his dad over that little trip he'd taken to Galveston!

Tony smiled and stomped on the gas. Hard.

23

This time it was Margaret who placed MacKenzie in her car seat. Margaret tried not to read anything in to it. After all, she was the one holding MacKenzie when Chloe asked for a ride to her trailer.

Like Chloe, MacKenzie seemed to have warmed-up to her and now, giggled and cooed when Margaret played Peek-a-Boo with her.

What Margaret wouldn't have given to see the adorable baby in something from one of the high-end baby boutiques back in Houston instead of the tattered thrift store-looking outfit on the precious little baby girl.

Chloe gave directions to her house and Margaret punched them into her car's GPS which made Chloe laugh and say "It's not that far."

"Want to make any stops on the way?" Margaret asked, hoping to stall so that she could spend more time with MacKenzie... and Chloe, of course.

"Well, I do need some things from the store but I'm not sure if I've got any money with me."

Margaret smiled. "Don't worry about that. I'd love to leave here, knowing you're all settled and have what you need."

Chloe bit her fingernail again, "Are you sure? I could use quite a bunch of stuff."

"That's fine. Now, which way is the closest grocery store?"

Chloe pointed the way with the sound of "Recalculating" in the background.

In a couple of minutes, they swung in the lot of *Big Foods*.

Once there, Chloe said, "I'll just get the necessities."

"Tell you what... I'll give you a credit card and you get everything you need while I stay in the car with MacKenzie."

"Just tell me how much I can spend and I promise not to go over."

"Get it all. Get whatever you need. Since the car's not going to be moving while you're in there, let's get MacKenzie out of her car seat and I'll bring her up here with me."

"Good idea."

As Chloe skipped toward the entrance, Margaret rolled down her window and yelled, "Chloe, get some baby toys if they have them. Okay?"

Chloe gave a nod as she disappeared into the store.

***

Paul cleared his desk, picked up his notebook and headed down the polished corridor for the last meeting of the day, stopping only to tell his secretary if his wife called to put her call through.

His secretary looked stunned. Paul never did that and this was an important meeting. In fact, the investors for a possible new stadium in Montreal were on their way up in the elevator. However, she nodded and made a mental note to do as her boss asked, no matter her private thoughts about it.

So, with a smile, she answered, "Sure thing."

"Don't forget." Paul replied as he walked away.

Paul felt better knowing if a call did come, he'd be contacted no matter his location in the building.

While he waited in the conference room, he dialed Margaret's cell phone again.

No answer. He hung up just in time to greet the group of investors. Many of whom he knew from past projects.

As the promotional film showed a state-of-the art three dimensional mock-up of possibilities for the stadium, no one would have guessed Paul's thought were on what it would take to pay a surrogate to carry a child for him and Margaret.

His mother always said "talk is cheap" and maybe it was. He needed to do the legwork to find out the "how" and "where" of it all. He already knew the "why".

24

Eventually, Chloe reappeared behind a grocery cart piled high with plastic bags, Margaret tucked MacKenzie in her car seat and sprung out to help Chloe put groceries on the other side of the back seat.

As they pulled out of the parking lot, a shiny white Cadillac pulled in.

Chloe let out a grasp. "Margaret, can you drive back across the lot?"

"Sure but I'll have to get turned around first. May take a moment to get back across in the traffic."

"Hurry. Okay?"

Margaret didn't answer. As soon as she got an opening in the traffic, she made a U-turn. When they re-entered the lot, a tall lanky guy with reddish hair practically bounced across the lot and into the store.

"We can go now," Chloe said in a low voice.

"Are you sure. We can wait here, if you want."

"I'm sure. Let's go."

Margaret looked back at MacKenzie and over to Chloe. She felt sure she'd just seen the father of MacKenzie. The resemblance couldn't be denied.

Tears that streamed down Chloe's face confirmed it.

In an effort to cheer the poor girl up, Margaret said, "Hey, why don't we drive through a fast food restaurant and take something home to eat?"

"*MY* home, you mean, don't you?"

"Of course."

"Well, in that case, I could eat something."

Margaret smiled. "Me, too."

Chloe returned Margaret's smile. "Eddie's gumbo is not the best this side of the Mississippi, is it?"

Margaret laughed. "No. Definitely not!"

They both were laughing so hard, it was difficult to be understood on the speaker at *Burger Joint*.

***

Ralph's radar gun was pointed at the evening rush hour traffic. He was surprised to see the gold Mercedes pull out of *Burger Joint*. The babe who drove it seemed more like "avocado and alfalfa" than a *Burger Joint* kind-of-gal.

He thought about pulling her over just to see her again but since she wasn't speeding, he'd look like a fool if he said something goofy like "I pulled you over because you didn't look like a greasy burger-kind of gal".

Even so, Ralph was curious why the girl was still in town and shifted to drive to follow her. Unfortunately, the rush hour traffic was so heavy, he couldn't pull off the lot in time to see which way she turned at the light.

In the end, he decided to return to the station. Second shift would be there soon and he could go home which would suit him just fine. The older he got, the less he roamed.

Ralph squared his shoulders, hoping there was a couple of thrills still to come in his life.

Later he thought, maybe he should have followed the gold Mercedes after all.

25

When Paul's secretary stopped by his office to make sure nothing else needed to be done and to say goodbye for the day, Paul was surprised that it was so late.

As he clicked off his computer, the sound of his cell phone made him jump and he had trouble keeping a note of disappointment out of his voice when he realized it was only a friend double checking the time for their racquetball game the following afternoon.

Paul called home for what seemed like the hundredth time that day. No answer, but he continued to cradle the phone even though it was unlikely Margaret was going to pick up.

Normally, Paul had little trouble making decisions but he was still undecided about what to do. Should he stay at his office which was an hour closer to Baton

Rouge or should he go home. Should he phone Margaret's parents or the highway patrol? Should he start driving toward Baton Rouge, looking for her along the way? Common sense told him not enough time had gone by for law enforcement to consider his wife missing. Worse, what if she didn't want to be found?

Paul walked down the hall to the conference room. He opened the humidor in the middle of the table and took out a cigar. He stuck it in his mouth, unlit and stood in front of the huge glass windows watching the lights of cars on the interstate and side streets below.

In Houston, gold Mercedes were a dime a dozen so even if he spotted one, he couldn't be sure it was her.

***

It was getting dark as Chloe directed Margaret past a restaurant, a hair salon and a run-down looking grocery store with bars on the windows before they turned down a gravel road.

Neither of them made idle chatter and Margaret thought Chloe looked sad and pensive.

As they rounded a small bend in the road, Chloe directed Margaret to pull in at the bottom of the driveway by her mailbox so she could hop out and check for her welfare check.

As soon as Chloe hopped out, MacKenzie woke up and let out a loud wail, probably from the sound of the car door being shut.

Margaret unfastened her seatbelt and twisted around to reassure the crying baby that all was well.

Chloe opened her mailbox and pulled out several envelopes. "Why don't you get MacKenzie out of the evening air and take her on up to the house. The key's under the mat."

Margaret peered up at the stars through her open car window and thought they'd never looked brighter. "Are you sure?"

"I'm sure." Chloe answered, standing in the dark.

Margaret reached for MacKenzie before she turned off the motor.

Chloe stayed at the mailbox reading her mail while Margaret found the key and entered the dilapidated trailer.

26

Paul unlocked his burgundy Porsche and slung his cell in the matching burgundy-leather passenger seat where he could grab it on the first ring.

As he guided his car out of the garage, he almost sobbed at the sound of an ambulance on the freeway. He prayed it wasn't some kind of omen as he headed toward home on the west side of Houston.

It was a wonder that he didn't cause an accident along the way because he was looking for Margaret's car back-and-forth across the lanes.

Fifteen minutes from the freeway, Paul's neighborhood decorative gate swung open when it sensed the electronic chip on his windshield.

As Paul maneuvered around a couple of early evening joggers, he found it hard to go the appropriate speed. Margaret may have come home, exhausted. Perhaps, she had fallen asleep and hadn't heard the phone.

When Paul finally make it home, his garage door opened to reveal nothing. No Mercedes. Only empty space. Even so, he still hoped maybe she'd been home and gone out again but after switching on a few lights and walking through the main floor, he knew that Margaret hadn't been back. Everything was exactly how he'd left it early that morning.

A sense of panic flooded his body as he tried to think of what to do.

Unfortunately, nothing came to mind.

Absolutely nothing.

27

Margaret placed MacKenzie in her crib with an old Teddy Bear and looked around for a box of diapers. There were none to be found so she'd have to leave the baby to go get the ones in the car.

As she opened the trailer's front door, Chloe motioned for her.

Near the mailbox, Margaret jumped with fright from a speeding flash of white, along with the frantic blare of a horn.

A screech of tires was followed by a dull thud as Chloe's body bounced off the mailbox and hit the ground.

Envelopes and papers from Chloe's hand seemed to float back toward the earth in slow motion.

Spinning car tires threw gravel in the air but when it settled down, the car was gone, leaving only a deathly quiet.

Margaret's arms and legs were jelly as she ran and bent down to the huddled mass lying in the weeds near the dented mailbox.

There, time seemed to stop.

The sound of the terrible, sickening dull thud kept repeating itself in Margaret's head. It was like hearing a vinyl record of the most horrible sound in the world play over- and-over again. Margaret desperately wanted someone to give the phonograph's needle a push.

Margaret knelt in the gravel and cradled Chloe like a limp rag doll.

Chloe mouthed one word: Tony.

Margaret felt Chloe's wrist for a pulse and found one - a very faint one.

She gently placed Chloe's body back on the grass, grabbed an envelope and sprinted for her car. Once there, she opened the door, grabbed her cell phone and shoved the envelope under her phone's flashlight app to see Chloe's address as she dialed for help. Luckily, there was service.

Although the 911 Operator wanted Margaret to stay on the line until help arrived, Margaret clicked "Call Ended" and ran to get MacKenzie, stopping only to pick up her cell phone that had slipped from her fingers and fallen to the ground.

Once again, Margaret knelt down by Chloe, turned on the cell's flashlight and laid it on the ground so that the young mother could see her baby for one last time in the fading twilight.

It was apparent that Chloe wanted to hold MacKenzie but the strength to do so wasn't there. So, Margaret held the squirming baby against Chloe as best she could.

Chloe's eyes fastened on Margaret and then flashed toward MacKenzie before closing for the last time.

Margaret slung her head back and screamed into the night sky.

Some things can only be lifted up with a scream from the depths of your soul and for Margaret, this was one of them.

Margaret's wail made MacKenzie cry and for this, Margaret was sorry and tried to comfort the baby but it was of little use.

A light breeze swirled around Margaret as she lifted MacKenzie from Chloe's body.

Margaret unfastened Chloe's heart necklace and placed it around MacKenzie's neck.

In one brief moment, Margaret had gone from a young woman to someone who felt like a hundred years old. She could barely walk back to the trailer but cries from the squirming baby in her arms were becoming more frantic.

Once inside, Margaret place the baby back in her bed and handed her a pacifier which seemed to comfort her enough so that she could go back to Chloe.

Against a backdrop of a soft siren that was getting louder, Margaret said "So, this is death" to the night air.

It was a nightmare to look down on a body that only moments earlier was full of hope and dreams. Now, it was gone with a flash of white paint and some shiny chrome.

Margaret sunk to the side of the road on her hands and knees. Vomit rolled uncontrollably from her throat.

Every so often, the wail of a baby cut through her misery.

Margaret wiped her eyes with her fingers and her nose on her sleeve.

After kissing Chloe on both cheeks, Margaret walked toward the sound of crying, picked up the baby and carried her back outside with her.

If a miracle happened, Chloe would get to see her baby one last time.

Chloe was in and out of consciousness, wondering if a gust of wind from Gabby was strong enough to make you feel like you'd been pushed.

Probably.

Maybe.

28

Ralph left the smallest pork chop for Tony. He figured Tony deserved it. It was a wonder that he, himself, had any appetite at all after listening to Estelle fuss and fume about Tony not making it home in time for dinner.

"When I was at Janie's this afternoon, I told Tony we'd be eating at seven sharp. That boy is always late!"

Ralph had to admit, Estelle was right. "When he is here, he's only here long enough to get more money... your car... or change his clothes."

"Janie dropped me off at the hospital and he was supposed to get my car back to me so that I could drive myself home but of course, he didn't."

Ralph reached for a toothpick. "How'd you get home?"

"I called a cab. Can you imagine? I ought to dock his allowance for the fare it cost me."

"Well, I tell you what, why don't the two of us eat the last two pieces of chocolate cake. He can do without."

Before Estelle had time to answer, Tony burst through the door, bouncing on one foot then the other.

"Tony, sit down and eat. You're making me nervous!"

"I'm not hungry, Mom. I've probably still got the flu or something."

"You seemed fine when you speeded away from Janie's earlier. I'm telling you that you'd better slow down... once and for all."

Tony slung himself down in a chair. "I've learned my listen."

"What do you mean by that?" Ralph questioned. "If you got another ticket, I'll know about it before I walk in the precinct door tomorrow."

Tony popped the top on a can of soda sitting by his plate. "I didn't get a ticket and I didn't mean anything. Just making small talk."

Ralph eyed Tony suspiciously.

Tony chewed his lower lip. "Okay, I'll come clean. I did brush the corner of the dumpster in the back parking lot at school today. You can barely see a dent but I promise I'll pay for the repairs."

152

"You bet you'll pay." Ralph shouted.

Ralph looked through the screen door. The car didn't look too bad. The dent could probably be popped-out and the front right fender would need a small paint job. Nothing much really.

In fact, Ralph was surprised that Tony was so upset. He'd caused more damage to Ralph's truck last year and wasn't near as upset about that as he appeared to be over Estelle's car.

"Maybe all my talks are finally getting through to him," Ralph whispered to Estelle as he moved past her to answer the phone.

Estelle took their plates to the sink as Ralph hung up the phone. "What was that about?"

"That was Harris. Hit and Run. Gotta go."

Ralph shoved the last of the chocolate cake in his mouth and gulped down his coffee before reaching for his hat.

29

Ralph ran his hand through his thin hair, popped a stick of gum in his mouth and turned on the overhead blue lights. When the stoplight ahead of him turned red, he inched forward, making sure no fool was going to run the light and the green lighters were aware of him. Only then, did he take off with his siren blaring.

Ralph hoped there wasn't going to be weeping and wailing when he got there. He wasn't good at comforting people. Never had been. He left that to the younger, more sympathetic cops; ones with an eye on promotions.

Yellow lights from a tow truck lit up his back window just as his tires hit a gravely road. Ralph wasn't surprised. Since the invention of police scanners, it was a race to see who'd make it to the scene first. "Oh well, they've gotta make a living, too," Ralph said to himself as he peered ahead to the blue light that flashed over a lifeless shape in the grass by the road.

As expected Harris was already there. The ambulance, too.

In his rear view mirror, Ralph saw Eddie from Buckley's jump down from the cab of the tow truck and run past him.

When Eddie sprinted to the motionless body, Harris stepped in front of him and held him from bending down to it.

With a huge yank of his whole body, Eddie escaped the hold Harris had on him.

Eddie slid down in the road and put his head in his hands. His wailing was loud with a shrill note of despair in it.

When the girl's body was lifted by paramedics, her hand dangled out from under the sheet, almost as if she was reaching back toward the trailer for something... or someone.

***

Paul zipped his pants and flushed the toilet. He grabbed a washcloth and ran it under the faucet before wiping his forehead. He was physically sick. It had been over twelve hours since Margaret left Baton Rouge. Hell, she could have made a round trip between the two cities in that amount of time.

He should have gone with her.

He should have cancelled his meeting or had someone else take over for him.

Every so often, he heard a car or thought he heard one. Either way, he ran to the window at the slightest sound. When he wasn't doing that, he was dialing some obscure town somewhere between Baton Rouge and Houston with the small hope that Margaret was stranded there with car problem. Anything else was unthinkable.

He'd make a few more phone calls to police stations along Margaret's route but he couldn't bear to start calling hospitals. Not yet.

The Houston police were gracious and took some information over the phone but basically, they told him not to call back for another twelve hours.

On his computer screen, he followed the path of his calls on a virtual map of Louisiana.

His eyes followed his trail of calls until they landed on the next dot. Lake Charles.

On the split screen, he searched for the police number there and dialed. No answer. That was strange. Didn't all police stations stay open twenty-four seven? Sure they did, he reasoned, unless there was a compelling reason for every cop to leave the station.

Paul told himself not to jump to conclusions. He'd wait awhile and try again.

Hopefully, Margaret would walk through the door before he dialed again.

30

Eddie stood by the mailbox with tears streaming down his face. Luckily, he'd stopped to eat at Sue's or he would have been way over near Lafayette when the call came over the scanner.

He'd had a feeling not to leave town but he never dreamed it would be because of something like this.

When Chloe's body was lifted by paramedics and her hand dangled out from under the sheet, Eddie felt the earth spin again. His knees buckled and he collapsed to the ground.

A loud wail started somewhere in the vicinity of his heart and worked its way out toward the heavens.

Eddie's future died along with Chloe and he knew it as surely as he knew his name.

He felt as if nothing or no one would ever matter from that moment forward.

It was only after the paramedics drove away that Eddie became aware of the noise. It was like a bell in the distance and it took him awhile to realize it was a baby's cry. Chloe's baby.

Eddie turned his body in the direction of the cry and there stood Margaret. MacKenzie in her arms.

***

Margaret shifted MacKenzie to her other arm. "Come on, grab my hand and I'll help you up."

Eddie reached out his hand. "What happened?"

"You fainted."

"Well that's a first." Eddie said as the memory of the outline of Chloe's body under the sheet hit him like a wave again and he fought not to lose consciousness for a second time. This time he won the battle.

Margaret let go of his hand when he stood and noticed for the first time a swipe of white paint smeared across Chloe's mailbox.

31

In all the commotion at the scene, Sheriff LeBlanc had taken another look at the gold Mercedes in the driveway. If anyone else had noticed the fancy car, they hadn't said anything.

Ralph made a mental note of the groceries on the backseat, as well as the baby's car seat. More than once, he opened his mouth to say something to Harris about giving the driver a ticket earlier but didn't.

He was unsure where this "hit and run" investigation was going to lead.

The fresh scrape across the mailbox was white. Pearly white.

He kept that to himself too, as he recorded the measurements Harris called out while pulling a tape from one end of a torn up gravel pit to the spot where Chloe came to rest.

No doubt the "hit and run" driver had been going too fast, judging from the skid marks on some crunched up gravel.

Ralph thought Harris had been uncharacteristically quiet throughout the entire event so he was glad when the last measurement was on paper and Harris got in his car and pulled away.

Ralph felt unsettled and didn't want to face the inquiring eyes of Estelle. He needed to get his thoughts straight before he was questioned about all of this.

Sue. He'd go there. She didn't question and she wouldn't seek any answers he wasn't ready to give... yet. Her kind of gossip was harmless, the "who makes the best pie dough" kind of stuff.

***

Paul backed the Porsche out of the garage and immediately drove right back in. What if Margaret came home and he wasn't here? What if she phoned home and he wasn't here to take the call? What if she sent someone to the house to get him? How would they find him?

What if... what if... what if Margaret didn't want to be found? Then what?

32

A gust of air carried Chloe skyward where a glowing bright light pulled her, much like a moving sidewalk, toward an effervescent group of colors.

As Chloe neared the colors, nestled among them was a host of faces, all familiar.

Amid the faces, hands reached out to touch and hug her.

Chloe looked over her shoulder at MacKenzie below but couldn't get any words to come out of her mouth. The best she could do was think a message of love and goodbye.

In reply, MacKenzie looked up, kicked both feet and raised her arms.

Flickering radiant light in front of Chloe distracted her from the fading baby in the arms of the lady back on the ground.

In front of Chloe, two large hands descended above the crowd. They cupped her face as a voice emancipating from the galaxy boomed "I will give you peace."

Immediately, Chloe's being was filled with joy like none other. The feeling was so intense multi-color flickers of light began to shine from her being.

***

Eddie reached for MacKenzie. "I feel like I need a glass of water and to sit down."

"Go ahead. I'll go get the groceries still in my car."

"Wait." Eddie handed MacKenzie back to Margaret. "Tell you what. Why don't you get me a glass of water while I go get the groceries?"

"Are you sure?"

"No problem."

"I thought you needed to sit down."

"I will in a moment."

Once the groceries were put away and MacKenzie was settled in her bed, Eddie said, "I'll be back. I want to see if my hunch is right about the white paint."

Margaret nodded.

"Margaret, there's something I need to know - good or bad, did Chloe say anything about me."

Seeing the pain etched on Eddie's face, Margaret replied, "All the time. She said you were the best friend she'd ever had and life wouldn't be the same without you."

As he left, Eddie beamed as he wept.

33

Harris wasn't surprised to see Sheriff LeBlanc's car when he got to work the next morning.

As he walked in the Sheriff's office, Harris immediately saw the calling card of the "hit and run" driver: a mailbox. It was on the floor.

Harris bent down and picked it up. "Want me to run this over to the lab to get a more precise paint color?"

Since Sheriff LeBlanc didn't answer, Harris continued, "A word to a few local auto body shops should just about wrap this whole unpleasant thing up."

The sheriff's large hands took the mailbox from Harris and put it back on the floor by his desk. "Let it go."

"What do you mean let-it-go?"

"Just what I said. Let it go!"

Harris was truly confused. "But..."

167

"I mean it. If you plan on making a career in law enforcement here in Lake Charles, you'll let it go."

As the pieces of the puzzle started to fit together, Harris slung himself in a chair across from the sheriff. "Not Tony. P-l-e-a-s-e not Tony."

Ralph didn't answer.

Harris tried to picture the good-looking, happy-go-lucky sheriff's kid in jail and knew the kid wouldn't last a day. He was too soft for what prison in Louisiana would have in store for him.

Ralph stood up and walked over to a window. "I've always done my duty and I've never failed to uphold the law but I can't put my own flesh and blood away for this stupid, careless, childish, terrible mistake. I can't. You understand it, don't you?"

Harris cleared his throat, wondering if the truth came out, he'd be considered an accessory to a crime.

The sheriff turned back around. "I need you, Buddy. I really do."

Harris decided that he could turn his head the other way. After all, people got by with crimes every day. But he wasn't so sure he'd ever be able to forgive himself for not standing up for the dead girl. "Ralph, I'm with you, but I sure feel sick about this whole thing."

"Well, if it makes you feel any better, Tony will be lucky if I don't kill him myself."

"I'm sure."

"As it is, I'm sending him to Morgan City this evening to go to work on an offshore rig. I guess leaving school, not graduating with his class, and not playing in the state championship will be some sort of punishment. I should have taken a firmer hand with him all along. I blame myself but I kept thinking he'd outgrow his wild ways. I was wrong."

"Knowing he'll be working his butt off is some sort of punishment," Harris reluctantly agreed.

"I haven't been the best dad in the world, nor the best husband either but I've been thinking that Estelle and I need to do some traveling and get away for a while. Besides, I'm much too old to raise a baby."

Harris struggled to absorb it all. So the rumors were right. The baby was Tony's.

Ralph wasn't sure what he would say or do once he got to the trailer but he had to get things settled before he went mad.

To Harris, he merely said, "I'll be back. Hopefully, sometime later today."

Harris didn't answer. He was already carrying the mailbox to the dumpster behind the station.

***

Margaret was impressed with the homey feeling within the trailer. Everything was sparkling clean. The furniture was a mixture of every possible style and screamed "garage sale items redone with love."

It was mid-morning before Eddie came back. The fact that Eddie let himself in with a key was not lost on Margaret, nor were the unmistakable signs that Chloe didn't live there alone.

As if sensing her need to know more, Eddie added, "We've lived here together since MacKenzie was born. Cheaper that way."

"Oh," Margaret said softly, noticing that Eddie was using the present tense as if Chloe was still alive. "Well, maybe I did know. I think Chloe told me in the car. But at the time, I wasn't paying attention. I expected to drop her off in Lake Charles and be on my way."

Margaret didn't say that things had changed now. Of course, she didn't have to say it. They both knew it.

MacKenzie batted the mobile that hung above her head on an electric baby swing that was gently slowing down.

MacKenzie whimpered and Eddie picked her up and glanced toward Margaret. "Let's get MacKenzie settled in her crib and then we can talk."

Eddie gently changed the baby's diaper and kissed her sleepy face.

Margaret ran her fingers across the baby angelic-looking face.

"Eddie, what about MacKenzie?" Margaret dared to ask.

From Eddie, there was no answer.

34

Surrounded by people from her past, Chloe's attention was on a pin-prick of light zig-zagging toward her.

As the light grew closer, the light's voice got louder. *"Intake. Make way. Intake."*

The faces, hands, and colors around Chloe melted away.

The pin-prick of light came to a stop in front of Chloe.

The once small brilliant light began to shift and form a dazzling array of colors that formed a human-like shape, much like an elderly grandmother with a clipboard in her hand. *"Welcome to the hereafter. We're glad you made it here, as we are with all of our residents. I'll be the one to get you settled-in."*

Chloe didn't speak as the figure shuffled through the papers on her clipboard.

"Now for a few basics. What kind of music do you want playing in your background?"

"What do you mean MY background?" Chloe wasn't sure, but it felt like beings were 'thought-to' instead of 'spoken-to'. When Intake answered, Chloe knew she was right.

"Not everyone wants to hear the same kind of music so we plug-in the kind of music you like in your personal background."

Chloe thought, *"But what if I get tired of it?"*

"Then, my dear, you only have to think me near and I'll make adjustments."

"Okay, then... what about some rock? It is permitted here?"

"Well, of course, as long as it doesn't disparage, incite or degrade anyone or anything."

"Okay, then... rock it is." In the background, Chloe heard her favorite 'Weird Guys' song.

Intake make a check on a sheet and turned the page.

"No, wait! I think I'd like to hear Clair de Lune by Debussy... or something by Rachmaninoff." Chloe wasn't sure how she knew to ask for either but when the first piano key sounded, her soul soared.

Turning another page, Intake asked, *"What kind of activity do you fancy?"*

"*I thought people who went to Heaven just floated around on clouds all day... or something,*" Chloe thought in reply.

"*Oh good gracious. I don't know where people get such silly ideas of heaven.*"

Chloe ignored Intake's last statement and answered "*What are my choices?*"

"*We have everything from Singing in the Angel Choir to adjusting auras.*"

"*Is there a list that I can choose from?*"

"*Sure. Follow me.*"

Chloe's somewhat humanoid form of endless colors swirled into a pinprick of white light at the same time as Intake's did.

Both dots of lights then zipped into a space that had automated scenes in front of them.

Chloe watched scenes of famous and non-famous writers as they chipped on stone tablets, dipped quill pens in ink, clicked away on typewriters, and hit keys on a keypad.

She watched cooks, some with chef hats on and some without. Some threw spinning dough in the air and some stirred fluffy batter of exquisite colors.

There were glass blowers forming flowers of glass, gardeners standing under enormous crops, and rows of rocking chairs filled with humanoid forms-of-color rocking smaller humanoid forms-of-color.

The scenes were endless.

175

Chloe knew the activity she wanted to do the moment it flashed before her. *"I want to paint."*

The split-second Chloe's thoughts left her mind, both she and Intake were no longer pinpricks of lights. They were back to their original humanoid shapes of color.

Intake put another check on her clipboard of papers. *"Good choice. Do you want to learn with the Masters or do something more up-to-date?"*

Chloe didn't know exactly the *kind* of painting she wanted to do, although she more-or-less knew the style and thought her words to Intake.

"Okay. Stay close. We have to zip through the golfers to get there. Always remember, when you want to do something different just think of me and I'll be back to get you reassigned. Oh, and good luck."

Chloe thought *"Thank you!"*

"Oh my twinkling stars! What am I saying! You don't need good luck here. After all, you made it here!

Chloe thought a smile to Intake.

And when you want to be with those you knew on earth, think me near and I'll take you there. Now, let's go get you with the other painters.

After darting above a sea of flying golf balls, Intake left Chloe at an easel in a meadow of bright poppies.

Surrounding Chloe were endless humanoid figures-of-color painting poppies.

Later, as Chloe made the last paint stroke, the entire swarm of colorful humanoids swirled together, landing in a meadow of wild horses and Texas Bluebonnets.

Chloe smiled and hummed a Debussy as the horses galloped and endless Texas bluebonnets swayed in the wind... and on her canvas.

Perfect.

Divine.

Heavenly.

35

Estelle wrapped her wet hair in a towel and stood in front of the bathroom mirror. She tried to avoid seeing new wrinkles and additional pounds.

What had happened to the young girl she'd been a long time ago. What had happened to the young girl who could eat anything-and-everything and never gain a pound? When had this middle-aged, overweight, wrinkly woman emerged? Was this her reward for fixing mouth-watering meals for everyone, including herself?

Estelle reached for her flannel bath robe and promised herself to start dieting and working-out.

Tomorrow.

Today, she'd be much too busy. She'd picked up an extra shift at the hospital for a volunteer away on vacation.

With a shrug, Estelle dressed and headed toward the kitchen. If she was going to get-going with losing weight, she needed to enjoy this last day of freedom.

Estelle opened the lid on her hiding place, the littlest canister, the one that said "Tea" and pulled out a chocolate bar to go with a Cola from the frig. What-the-heck did she care. No one else really did. Besides, Ralph had left early, almost before daylight so there was no one to see her "Breakfast of Champions".

Candy bar in hand, Estelle swung open the kitchen door to the carport for some fresh air before the Texas heat and humidity made that impossible for the day. When she did, a gust of wind nearly blew her down.

Through the screen door, she made a startling discovery. There was a swipe of paint missing from the front passenger side of her car and what looked like a small dent.

Estelle let out a shriek. "Tony!"

Estelle whirled around and marched to the bottom of the stairs where she met Tony bounding down them, two at a time.

"Calm down, mom. I already told you about the car."

"I will *not* calm down. It's a lot worse than you lead me to believe, Tony? What did you do?"

"Mom, I'm in trouble. Big trouble."

Seeing Tony worried face and teary eyes, Estelle took pity. It was only a car after all. "I'm not happy but the car can be fixed. Of course, you're gonna pay for it."

"Mom, you don't get it. I'm in BIG TROUBLE. There were two girls at the mailbox when I rounded the curve. Then… there was only one… still standing."

Estelle reached for the banister rail to steady herself. If this was some kind of sick joke, she was going to clobber the kid – for real.

"Please tell me this is a joke!" Estelle screamed. He had to be kidding. She'd put him in therapy for doing this to her. He must be cracking up. Maybe it was a head injury that had gone undetected since football season.

Estelle's stomach churned. She glanced up at Tony with a sick feeling in the pit of her stomach. "Please tell me this is a joke. Please…"

Tears rolled down Tony's face.

"Who?" Estelle stuttered.

"The mother of my baby, that's who." Tony screamed. "That's who."

The girl with the baby at Buckley's flashed before Estelle's eyes and she sobbed.

"Mom, I've done something not even you and your Beaudreau money can fix! Life is over for me!"

A look of terror spread across Estelle's face. Her body swayed. She let-go of the banister to steady herself better against the frame of the kitchen door but before she reached it, the horrible realization of Tony's revelation penetrated, her knees buckled and Estelle sunk down in a heap on the floor.

Tony fell to the floor and cradled his aging mother as he poured forth the whole story.

Estelle was shocked and sickened by what had happened.

She was consumed by grief for the girl she had never met.

She was devastated for the girl's baby – Tony's baby, too.

She was deeply sorrowed for her son. His life would never be the same.

Estelle wanted it all to be a lie.

She wanted to rewind time and fix this for Tony... but how?

This wasn't like sewing on a button.

This wasn't like driving forgotten homework to school.

This wasn't like bandaging a cut.

THIS WAS DIFRFERENT!

Tony was right.

Money couldn't fix everything.

In the past, Beaudreau money had always been the answer.

Today was the first time in Estelle's entire life she felt utterly helpless.

36

Eddie grabbed a beer from Chloe's frig and settled himself in the shabby recliner.

Margaret lowered herself on the lumpy sofa and stared at a painting on the opposite wall.

It was a poorly done painting, an amateurish attempt to portray a galloping horse with a few Texas bluebonnets scattered at its feet. It wasn't the kind of painting that Margaret would have usually noticed.

Now, for some unexplained reason, Margaret found the painting utterly fascinating and couldn't take her eyes off of it. It was as if she had fallen down the rabbit's hole where everything was contorted and unexpected.

Since Eddie seemed lost in thought, Margaret stood and walked over to the painting to get a better look.

"She painted it." Eddie said before taking another swig of beer.

"Chloe?"

"Yeah, Chloe. She liked to paint. I bought her the canvas and some paints for Christmas last year."

Margaret pulled her attention from the painting and looked at Eddie. "You're a good man, Eddie. A real good man."

Before Margaret sat back down on the sofa, a knock on the door startled her. Eddie didn't move to answer it so Margaret opened the door.

Margaret was surprised to see the Sheriff LeBlanc again and stepped aside for him to enter. With his hat in his hands, he said, "Eddie, I'm really sorry."

"You've got a lot of nerve coming here," Eddie said as he got up and sauntered to the refrigerator for another beer.

Eddie sat down at the old Formica table in the cramped kitchen adjacent to the living room.

The sheriff tossed his hat to the sofa and joined Eddie at the table. "Wouldn't mind a beer or two either."

"Get it yourself."

"Eddie, I know you're hurtin' bad."

186

"Like I said, you're got a lot of nerve coming here. In fact, I've got half-a-mind to shoot you and that idiot son of yours, too."

"Now, Eddie, you've got no proof."

"I bet that proof is sitting in your carport. Besides, who else would be flying around this part of town in a white caddy? Maybe someone who was high most of the day, skipped school to start running-the-roads, and was looking for someone to party with before the rest of the high school girls were back out for the night?"

Sheriff LeBlanc opened the refrigerator and pulled out a beer. "You're crazy. You ain't got no proof."

"Really? Why don't we march down to the high school and do a check of the attendance records today?"

Sheriff LeBlanc took a long sip of beer. "Well, so what? What would that prove?"

"Did I mention that I saw your precious kid zipping past Buckley's this afternoon in your wife's caddy?"

"Doesn't prove he was at the wheel."

Eddie laughed. "I think if a jury put all the pieces together, along with my eye-witness account, they'd come to the same conclusion as me."

The sheriff finished his beer and crushed the can in his hand. "Suppose you're right. What good is ruining more lives going to do? Won't bring her back, son, and I doubt she'd want more lives ruined."

Eddie glared at the sheriff. "What do you or your precious family know about Chloe? Nothing. So don't act like you know or even try to guess what she might or might not want to happen. You know nothing."

"You're right, Eddie. I'm just a poor, middle-aged man in a one horse town and I sure as heck don't have all the answers. But this I do know, breaking another heart, won't fix yours."

Tears rolled down Eddie's face as he answered. "You're watching a heart breaking right now when you're looking at me."

The sheriff walked over and placed his hand on Eddie's shoulder. "I'm sorry, Eddie. Truly, I am."

Eddie gave a slight nod as tears rolled down his face. "Hell, you know I'm not going to force it. Who'd believe a grease monkey against the town sheriff anyway?"

Sheriff LeBlanc lifted his hand from Eddie's shoulder. "Thank you."

"I'm assuming you're picking up the tab for all the medical bills; burial ones, too."

The sheriff opened the trailer door before answering. "Of course."

"I want things nice. No skimping on plot or headstone. Okay?"

"You've got my word" was the last thing Sheriff LeBlanc said as he struggled to shut the door against the occasional strong gust from Gabby.

As the door shut, MacKenzie whimpered from her bedroom and Margaret sprinted to be near her, worried.

Even though the baby was given to her by Chloe in the split-second before she was gone for good, the formality of taking the baby from a grieving boyfriend and a gruff sheriff was another matter.

How does one ask for a baby?

How does one ask for a life?

How does one ask for happiness in the midst of another's misery?

Margaret felt unsure and inadequate.

For the first time since becoming involved in this situation, Margaret wished Paul was with her. He'd know how to handle this unexpected event. Unfortunately, there was far too much to explain for her to call him now.

37

As he walked into his office, the sheriff brushed aside a cellophane wrapped piece of cherry pie, obviously a gift from Sue.

He motioned for Harris to get off the phone. "Did I miss anything?"

Harris picked up Ralph's piece of pie and pulled a plastic fork out of his top desk drawer. "Yes, in fact, you did."

"What? I don't have all day."

Harris popped a forkful of pie in his mouth. "A Mr. Paul Sinclair called to see if the Sheriff's Department had any information on his wife, Margaret. Seems she's traveling from Baton Rouge to their home in Houston and hasn't been heard from for over a day."

Ralph let out a soft whistle.

"Oh, did I mention she's in a Mercedes? A GOLD Mercedes."

"What did you tell him?"

"That I'd check around and for him to stop here when he arrives."

Ralph felt his face flush. "What do you mean when he arrives?"

"He's heading our way, looking for her. Do you reckon that gold Mercedes we saw at the 'hit-and-run' last night could be her?"

"Of course, you know it is… but keep all of this between the two of us for now. Understand?"

"I figured as much," Harris said, taking another bite of cherry pie.

"And Harris, get on the computer and run a background check on Margaret Sinclair of Houston. A 'Mr. Paul Sinclair', too. Find out all you can."

"Is there anything in particular you're looking for?"

"Yes, finances… and stability."

This time it was Harris who let out a soft whistle.

38

Paul was halfway to Lake Charles. He should be there in a little over an hour. Usually, music blasted from his radio but today, he rode in silence.

In his mind, Paul kept mulling over his phone conversation with the Lake Charles police department. The policeman sounded like he was on the verge of saying more before their conversation ended.

Paul was worried. Things didn't add up. He had always known where to find Margaret every moment of every day since they'd married. Not calling him was totally out of her character.

Margaret was not the kind of person to cause him, or anyone to worry needlessly. This wasn't to say that Paul never worried about her. Mainly, he worried that she would never be really happy unless they had a family.

Paul remembered another trip several years ago. He and Margaret were traveling through Lake Charles on their way to Mardi Gras in New Orleans when Margaret suddenly felt ill. They had just crossed the Lake Charles Bridge when Margaret asked Paul to pull over.

They parked along Lakeshore Drive and Margaret hung her head out of her open door and vomited. They both assumed she was finally pregnant. Feeling ecstatic, they had driven on to the Big Easy and celebrated in style.

It was not until they returned to Houston that it became apparent Margaret was not pregnant after all.

As the miles clicked away on the flat highway from Texas to Louisiana, Paul opened his moon roof and hit the gas, wondering what could possibly make Margaret forget everything and act so irrational.

Speeding past the exit ramp to the town of Vinton, the answer hit him full force: a baby.

Paul's spirit soared. Margaret had found them a baby. It had to be that. Nothing else made sense.

Paul floored the gas and watched the accelerator needle shoot higher on the dash.

39

Estelle rather liked the uniform all hospital volunteers wore on duty, although it was hard to fasten the snap on the neck.

Usually, Ralph fastened it for her but he still hadn't come in from work so she yelled for Tony. "Tony, come here. I need you."

Tony appeared, eyes still red from crying most of the day, "Whatcha need mom?"

"Help me with the snap on the back of this uniform. I'm heading to the hospital. I'm not taking my Cadillac out of the carport until I talk to your dad. Call a cab for me."

"Sure thing."

"I'm not locking up the keys to my car but after all that's happened, I hope you've learned your lesson. Promise not to leave here."

Tony nodded. "I promise."

***

While waiting on Eddie's reply to her unspoken question, Margaret was playing with MacKenzie in a sandbox behind the trailer when Eddie yelled out the window. "The hospital called. Someone needs to sign some papers and I'd like for you to go with me."

Unexpectedly, a sob escaped Margaret and all she could do was nod as she picked up MacKenzie and went inside to pack a diaper bag.

***

Ralph knew he hadn't always kept his word. After all, there was that week in Galveston with Sue, but today he was determined to keep the promise he'd made to Eddie.

Ralph wasn't sure how to go about paying the girl's hospital bill. Luckily, he'd gone to school with several of the present hospital administrators and he was reasonably sure, he could count on one of them to help him figure it out and most importantly, keep their mouth shut.

Of course, this kind of thing needed to be done in person.

So, he radioed Harris he'd be out of the office for a while.

40

The blue flashing lights seemed to come out of nowhere. Paul couldn't believe his luck! Okay... yes, he was speeding. But of all times to get a ticket, this was the worse.

Paul needed to reach Margaret and this would slow him down. He hoped the lanky officer approaching his car would hurry it up.

Paul knew he'd better adjust his attitude. He didn't want to end up in jail for some trumped-up charge.

Finally, the officer approached his car. "My name is Deputy Harris and I've pulled you over for speeding. Do you know that you were going eighty-eight in a seventy zone?"

"I'm sorry sir."

"Well, this is going to cost you. I need to see your license and proof of insurance."

Paul handed both to the deputy who immediately let out a low whistle. "I'll be right back."

Back in the squad car, Harris radioed the sheriff. He'd want to know the girl's husband had made it that far.

The line was full of static. Harris couldn't be sure but he thought the sheriff said "haul him in" so he did.

41

A shiny gold Mercedes, a run-down looking cab and a squad car pulled into the hospital parking lot at the same time.

It took a minute for things to settle in the minds of Sheriff LeBlanc, Estelle LeBlanc, Eddie Smith and Margaret who was holding a baby in her arms, but when they did, Estelle suggested that they take the elevator to the hospital chapel on the fourth floor.

Inside the elevator, Margaret was shocked when she glanced at her reflection in the mirrored doors. Her face was ashen white and her eyes looked like someone had circled them with a black marker. She attempted to smooth her thick, wavy hair back out of her face.

Eddie looked like he was slightly drunk.

The sheriff looked years older than when Margaret first encountered him only a day ago.

The lady, who introduced herself as Estelle, the sheriff's wife, had a worried look.

When the doors unexpectedly opened on third, Margaret fought the urge to jump off with MacKenzie and run away from the group, but she stayed.

When the group got out on fourth, Estelle said, "Go down the hall all the way to the door at the end. I'm going to pop into the children's waiting room to grab a few toys for the baby to play with while the rest of us talk."

It didn't take long for Estelle to return and for the group to get settled in small wooden pews.

Usually, one to keep quiet, Margaret felt a need to speak first. "I have something to say that may or not sway any of you but it is the truth and I want each of you to know it. Chloe's car broke down on the interstate this side of Baton Rouge and she needed a ride. The two of us formed a bond and right before she closed her eyes for the last time, she gave her baby to me. You may not believe me but it is the truth. I want this baby and I promise to raise her like my own. I will keep her safe and she will be loved. I have no other kids but even if I should one

202

day, this baby will be as fiercely loved. Always."

Sheriff LeBlanc nodded toward Margaret. "I'm going to be quite honest here. I did a background check on both you and your husband. I can vouch that you have the means to raise a baby and both of you are stable people."

Margaret reached over a pew and hugged the sheriff. "Thank you. I won't disappoint you... or Chloe."

Estelle walked to the altar at the front of the room and sat down on the floor where MacKenzie was playing with the toys she'd brought to her. "I would love for this precious baby, my beautiful granddaughter, to have a wonderful life with a couple who would cherish and love her. Always. If I were younger, I'd raise her myself. But both Ralph and I are too old."

Margaret stood and walked to the front of the room and hugged Estelle. Only then did Margaret look at Eddie, unsure of what he would say.

Eddie wanted to say "no" but decided in the end he needed to think a few minutes before answering.

He decided not to tell the group that Chloe had been looking into adoption agencies and they'd spent hours trying to figure out how to afford all the things a baby needed. Baby food, clothes, doctor visits, etc. Just the cost of diapers was straining their meager budget to the point that something had to be done.

Eddie also knew Chloe would want him to realize his dream of owning his own auto garage, complete with his own tow truck. Not only would that take money, it would mean log days with little, if any, time to raise a little girl.

Even if all of it wasn't true, which it was, Eddie knew he couldn't fight the Beaudreau family if Tony took a fancy later to raising MacKenzie.

With what he knew, he could probably send Tony to jail but what good would that do? It certainly wouldn't bring Chloe back and truthfully, the whole thing really did look like an accident, pure and simple.

Estelle spoke up, "If it will make you feel any better, we're sending Tony to work off-shore which is probably as good as sending him to jail and we plan to pay for Chloe to be buried at that sweet little cemetery on the other side of the Lake Charles Bridge, the one right outside of Sulphur."

Eddie nodded.

Estelle continued, "Now, what can we do for you, son?"

Eddie thought for a moment. He hated any of this being about money but when it came down to Chloe's wishes, his future was part of them. "Me? I've always fancied owning my own station."

Estelle wanted to click her heels. She'd saved her son. Oh, sure, she had to make some concessions that she really didn't want to make but Tony was worth it. Besides, Tony would have to live with his conscious and Janie and her husband could count on living in the Governor's Mansion. At most, there would be a small piece in the paper about a hit-and-run and Estelle would have to take a taxi around town until it was safe to get her car fixed.

Estelle opened her purse and took out her checkbook, asking Eddie if he'd be willing to take installments instead of one lump sum. He was.

Afterwards, Ralph and Estelle took turns carrying MacKenzie back to the parking lot.

Once there, Ralph turned to his wife and said, "Guess I'll head back to the station if you're going to stay here until your shift is over."

Estelle nodded. "Life does go on, whether we want it to or not. I'll stay."

"Call me when you're done. No need to phone a cab."

Estelle broke out in a huge smile before turning to go back inside.

Eddie put MacKenzie in her car seat and hopped in the passenger side for a ride back to Chloe's trailer. "Thanks for giving me a ride back to Chloe's trailer... well, I guess it's *my* trailer now. What do you think?"

Margaret padded him on his knee. "She'd want you to have it. She talked about you all the time. And Eddie, there's something there of Chloe's I'd like to have..."

Eddie smiled. "I'll go take it off the wall."

Margaret nodded.

The horse painting would be perfect in a certain little girl's room.

Always.

42

Back on the highway, Margaret broke into a cold sweat when blue lights flashed behind her.

Margaret pulled to the side, knowing leaving with MacKenzie was too good to be true. They'd come for the baby, no doubt.

It was Harris who walked to her door.

"I knew this would happen and they'd change their minds," Margaret wailed.

"I don't know what you're talking about but there's someone who wants to see you."

At first, the Louisiana sun was so bright, Margaret couldn't make out the shadowy figure that emerge from the car that pulled in behind the squad car.

Then she knew.

It was *him.*

Of course.

EPILOGUE

Traveling with a twelve-year-old brother was no picnic for any eighteen-year-old girl, but by evening, she'd be at her grandparent's house for dinner and back on campus before the freshman dorm curfew.

With any luck, she would get there earlier and she and her LSU friends could go out, if only for an hour or two.

The trip had taken longer than usual due to heavy traffic and road construction outside of Houston.

Of course, there was still the strange Lake Charles "ritual" to get through.

Every year, on the same date, her family pulled in at the same gas station.

As they glided to a stop this year, the girl made a mental note that the old yellow neon sign that flashed "Eddie's" had been replaced with a digital and larger one on a post high above three shiny tow trucks.

When her brother bolted for the building and the candy racks, her dad followed. On cue, two mechanics appeared to clean their windows and check the oil.

It was the only station where the girl had ever seen people do this. Yet, her parents acted like it was quite normal. It was usually at this point, an elderly, sweet lady would appear with something for her — a book or box of homemade treats.

When the girl was younger she thought the whole thing was sweet.

Now, it seemed rather weird.

Sweet, but weird.

***

In her empty front room, Queenie DuBois shook chicken bones from her velvet bag.

Only the wishbone fell in the circle of red.

It was then that the *Psychic Queen of the Bayou* knew that when she passed, her spirit would be at rest because she had finally moved past the worse and saddest reading of her entire life.

***

Eventually, the expensive car glided away and Ralph unzipped the navy jacket with *Eddie's Tow and Service* printed on it that he put on once every year. He lowered his sunglasses and wiped a tear from his eye while he waited for Estelle to emerge from behind the counter.

Eddie had quit taking money from Estelle and him years ago. Even so, there wasn't much left now due to Tony's never ending legal woes, not to mention the money it took to put Janie and Archer in the governor's mansion years ago.

As soon as Ralph and Estelle left, Eddie hung up his jacket and walked around to his truck parked out back.

He bent down and ran his hand through the grass near his building where there always seemed to be a gentle wind. When he stood up, he was clutching a small bunch of sweet clover.

Eddie thought it was a small miracle that he could always find patches of clover blooming there.

No matter the season.

No matter the weather.

Eddie's heart was at peace as pulled off of the lot and hurried toward the cemetery in Sulphur.

He had a lot to tell and Chloe would be anxious to know every detail as soon as he got there.

Books by
Nancy Cadle Craddock
can be found on Amazon.

Signed copies can be requested
using the "Contact Me" link at
NancyCadleCraddock.com

Winsley Walker

Beneath the Paint

Liars

Saving Tattoo

Lullaby of Lake Charles

Made in the USA
Charleston, SC
17 August 2016